BETWEEN WORLDS: A GAMER'S ODYSSEY

ASHLEE MACK

Made with ♥ on the Notion Press Platform
www.notionpress.com

To all the gamers all over the world!

Contents

ACKNOWLEDGEMENTS

To my dear friends, thank you for your constant support, laughter, and belief in me. And to my beautiful girlfriend, whose love, strength, and inspiration sparked the heart of this story, this book exists because of you. I'm endlessly grateful.

I

A Gamer's Haven

The Digital Distraction

His fingers moved swiftly over the controller, almost as if they were enchanted. Ashlee sat cross-legged on the floor of his Guangzhou apartment, bathed in the flickering blue light of the television screen. His unkempt brown hair fell into his eyes as he leaned forward, wholly absorbed, watching his character battle yet another enemy in Elden Ring. A forest of gaming consoles surrounded him, casting shifting patterns of light and shadow that painted the walls and ceiling like a virtual world spilling over into the real one. The sound of Julia opening the door broke his trance. She stood there, framed by the faint city lights from outside, arms crossed, and a look that spoke volumes before she said a word.

"You're still at it, Ashlee?" she sighed, her voice a mix of fatigue and frustration. "When will you face real life?"

Ashlee paused, but only for a moment. "I'm actually catching up with Tim and Ashley online—it's social enough," he replied, eyes never leaving the screen. His thumbs flicked expertly, almost as if to underline his point.

Julia took a step into the room, letting the door click shut behind her. The sound seemed to echo in the small space. She dropped her purse on the couch, the movement full of resigned energy. "Social enough for whom?" she asked, moving closer, her shadow crossing over the screen.

"For me," Ashlee said, tilting his head slightly to see past her. "And for Tim and Ashley too, I imagine. We're coordinating a raid here."

Julia rubbed her temples, trying to massage away the day's stresses. "And what about me, Ashlee? Or the rest of your life?"

Ashlee glanced at her, the eerie glow from the screen making his face seem otherworldly. "You make it sound like I'm abandoning ship or something," he said, half chuckling. "I'm just—well, I'm engaged, you know?"

She folded her arms tighter, her expression softening just a bit as she watched him, so engrossed. The distance between them felt as much a part of the room as the clutter and cables. "It'd be nice if you were a little more engaged in reality sometimes."

"I'm perfectly in touch," Ashlee replied, missing the sarcasm in her voice. His eyes darted to the screen and back to her. "We could have dinner later. I'll order in?"

Julia sighed, a soft sound almost swallowed by the hum of electronics. "Like every night this week?" She walked over to the window, gazing out at the vast city, where distant neon lights mirrored the chaos of his virtual adventures. "I've got meetings first thing, Ashlee. I'm just so—so tired of this."

Ashlee pressed a button on the controller, making his character take a defensive stance. He tried to sound more earnest, but the game called too insistently for his attention. "Okay, maybe I can log out after this session," he said, half-believing it himself. "Then we can talk?"

Julia watched him for a moment longer, searching for something in his expression, something that wasn't there. "If you're done by then," she murmured, her voice almost drowned out by the sound of explosions on the TV.

Her gaze lingered on him, slouched over the controller, as if imprinting the scene into memory. It felt like something they'd lived through a hundred times, and she knew exactly how it ended. She turned and headed to the bedroom, the sound of her footsteps disappearing down the hall.

Alone, Ashlee exhaled, relieved yet strangely unsettled. The dialogue boxes from Tim and Ashley filled the side of the screen, urging him to focus. He leaned in, trying to lose himself again in the game, trying to ignore the tension that still buzzed through the room, more persistent than any boss he'd faced all night.

Reflections in the Glow

The soft, rhythmic pulse of the electronic hum was like a lullaby to Ashlee's senses, but not quite enough to lull him to sleep. He lay in bed, staring at the ceiling, still lit by the pale glow of his idle gaming rig. Beside him, Julia shifted restlessly in her sleep, her brow furrowed even in dreams. Ashlee blinked slowly, feeling the adrenaline of the game still tingling in his fingertips, images of bosses and battlefields looping behind his eyes like a cinematic reel. He exhaled, long and deep, trying to release the tension of the evening. It didn't work.

The room was otherwise silent, save for the occasional murmur of wind against the window, an accompaniment to his wide-eyed solitude. Ashlee turned onto his side, facing the dark shape of the monitor, its lights blinking lazily as if mocking his inability to let go. His body lay in bed, but his mind wandered back to the treacherous digital landscapes he'd just traversed. It was as if the excitement of the game had wrapped itself around him like an invisible cloak, hard to shake off even in the comfort of his own bed.

He closed his eyes, but it only made the images sharper. Fiery dragons, towering bosses, and the gleam of virtual loot all swam in vivid detail. His fingers twitched with phantom sensations, eager for the familiar grip of the controller. A bead of sweat traced a line down his temple, and he wiped it away, opening his eyes to find the real world still there, expectantly waiting.

Julia let out a soft sigh, rolling over to face him. Her eyes stayed shut, but the tension in her expression was visible even in the dim light. She murmured something, indistinct, but it carried the same weight as her earlier words. It was a small sound, but to Ashlee, it felt like an unbridgeable chasm between them.

Ashlee's thoughts looped back to their conversation. He heard Julia's voice again, clear and insistent, challenging him to step out of the game and into reality. The question of when he'd face real life echoed louder than the boss fights he couldn't quite banish from his mind. Her frustration was familiar, like the soundtrack to his evening rituals, but it struck a different chord tonight, a little more real and a little less escapable.

He turned onto his back again, staring once more at the ceiling. The same four cracks he'd been staring at since they moved in seemed to form patterns he'd never noticed before. His head throbbed gently with the transition from frenetic gameplay to stillness, from a hero battling monsters to a man battling sleep and the doubts of his wife.

It wasn't that Ashlee didn't care about Julia's concerns. He did. But the pull of the game, the thrill of it—it was a world where he knew his place, where everything had rules, even if they were punishing. Out there, in the world beyond the glow of his screens, everything felt messier. The thought tugged at him, even as he struggled to hold onto the victories he'd scored that night.

His breathing slowed as he tried to calm the storm inside. The room was warm, a stark contrast to the chill of his silent battles. Julia's presence was a solid line of heat beside him, and he could almost convince himself that the distance was imagined, that they'd find a way to bridge it once morning came.

But morning felt far off, and sleep even further. Ashlee rolled to his other side, careful not to disturb her, and stared again at the blinking lights. They seemed to beckon him, a siren song of challenges left unfinished and friends left waiting. His eyelids felt heavy, but not with sleep—just with the weight of knowing how wide the gap had become.

Julia turned again, pulling the blanket tighter around her, her body curling into a question mark that Ashlee felt he had no easy answers for. He sighed again, closing his eyes once more, willing them to stay shut this time, hoping that maybe he'd wake to find it was all just part of a passing dream.

II

The Dream Begins

Awakening in Armor

Swallowed by sheets and dreams, Ashlee sank into the sleep of a gamer who spent too much time in other worlds. An imagined wind chilled his skin, and almost immediately he was in it. Here, he wore metal, not cotton, and he was the brave, skilled hero of his favorite video game. Instead of hesitating, Ashlee welcomed this transformation. Every breath was ragged, every step was sure, and every detail was realer than real. The stone floor felt gritty underfoot, his sword was firm in his hand, and his enemy was larger than life. A fearsome roar filled the castle corridor as sparks and adrenaline flew. The monster's slashing attacks brought both Ashlee and his armor to their knees. When the imagined pain became too much, the dream shattered like a brittle bone. A moment later, he was awake, his head pounding and his skin clammy with sweat.

The day had been long, and the bed in Ashlee's Guangzhou apartment was nearly too short. It seemed a single strand of his unkempt hair reached the wall while his feet hung clear off the edge of the mattress. With a yawn that pulled every ounce of oxygen from the room, he unceremoniously plopped himself onto the plain white sheets. Sleep descended faster than expected. The bed swallowed him as quickly as his everyday responsibilities did, pulling him down through layers of fatigue and exhaustion. For a moment, his mind teetered on the edge of wakefulness. He was conscious of the noises in the streets below, and he hoped he had enough energy left to sleep soundly. Then, in an instant, it was gone.

The familiar chill of an imagined breeze coursed through Ashlee, and he was no longer in his modest bedroom. Instead, he was inside a vivid dream. Here, the cold was welcome, the weight was welcome, and the transformation was welcome. His light sleeping shirt was replaced by gleaming metal armor. It covered every inch of him, and he relished the feel of its protective shell against his skin. Here, he was the bold and daring hero of Elden Ring, and instead of hunching like a man who spent all day hunched over a keyboard, he strode forward with the commanding gait of a man with nothing to lose. The space was charged with anticipation, and Ashlee moved through it with the absolute confidence of someone who had been here many times before.

This was a dream, but it was realer than real. Every sensation echoed through his imagined self, amplifying his awareness until the waking world was a distant memory. Ashlee drew in deep, labored breaths. They felt more alive than anything he'd breathed outside this place. The cool metal that covered him rattled with his every motion, and instead of hesitating, Ashlee delighted in it. In his right hand was a sword, impossibly heavy but completely steady. It was perfect. Everything was perfect. Ashlee's fingers wrapped around the hilt as if they'd been waiting to hold it his whole life.

He explored the crumbling castle corridor with precise movements that showed not a trace of doubt. With each step, Ashlee's armored boots crunched grit and debris against the stone floor. His heart pumped furiously with the sheer thrill of it all. Adrenaline and assurance powered him forward, and a sly smile took over his face. He was deeply, truly here, and he noticed every flickering shadow that danced across the castle's vast walls.

A dream monster loomed, larger than life and filling the air with palpable danger. A lesser hero would have shrunk away in fear, but Ashlee was no lesser hero. His breath came quicker. He welcomed the boss's immense silhouette with open arms and bated breath. The anticipation made his heart beat faster and harder, and his only concern was how much more excitement it could handle. This was the fight he'd been longing for.

The beast let out a terrifying roar as it closed in. It was so close and so loud that the castle shook, rattling Ashlee's armor with convincing force. He could almost feel the vibrations inside his body, jostling his bones. Ashlee squared himself to the beast, letting the rush of it overtake him. The corridor was illuminated by flying sparks as his sword clashed against the enemy's armor. The energy was tremendous, and Ashlee parried and swung with a mastery he had never known in real life. He imagined this was the way pro athletes must feel on the best day of their careers.

The clash of metal rang through the space, drowning out everything but Ashlee's labored breaths and his enemy's determined, unforgiving attacks. It was better than any game, better than any waking experience, better than anything Ashlee had known. He moved his avatar with such precision and force that he half expected the monster to bow out early. He wondered, in a tiny corner of his mind, if a dream would ever let him win this quickly. The more the possibility tugged at him, the more determined he was to finish the fight. The air felt thin and brittle, ready to shatter at any moment. Ashlee breathed it in, feeling the climax of it all teeter just beyond his reach.

The monster drew nearer and nearer, closing the space between Ashlee and his own raw desire. A powerful slashing attack brought him to his knees, but still Ashlee kept his focus on the prize. He felt the full weight of armor and urgency bear down on him as the imagined pain brought him closer to a finish than he had ever been before. He took another ragged breath, his every ounce of attention straining for the decisive moment, and the dream splintered like a too-thin branch. It was an explosion of one's and zero's, and Ashlee was suddenly awake.

The walls of his small apartment closed in with every staccato thump of his heart. Ashlee's skin was clammy, and his pulse was unsteady. His whole being wanted to be back in the castle. The adrenaline from his dream-life lingered like an extended echo, refusing to settle. Ashlee lay perfectly still, drenched in sweat and excitement. When he was sure he was alone and awake, he let out a long, slow breath. Part of him was glad to be back. Part of him wasn't.

Aftermath of a Virtual Odyssey

The first rays of sun came through Ashlee's bedroom window, bathing the messy room in a warm, forgiving glow. If not for the light and the chill of waking reality, Ashlee might have believed he was still in the dream. His heart was still pounding, his skin was still damp, and his hands still moved with adrenaline-fueled precision. In a flash of understanding, Ashlee knew the dream was more than just a dream. It was training. He rushed to his high-end PC, hardly noticing that the sound of morning traffic had replaced the deafening roar of his dream monster. He booted up Elden Ring with trembling fingers. At once, his movements were flawless. His hands were sure. It was as if he was still in the dream.

With the early sun filtering in, the bedroom was much less bleak than it had been the night before. Clothes were strewn about the floor. A few open soda cans lined the small desk. Dust covered the monitor, and one of the curtains was crooked, but in this light, the mess almost seemed charming. If Ashlee squinted just right, he could even imagine that he'd arranged it this way on purpose.

He stood and took it all in, still not quite believing the dream was over. It had been so real. More real than anything in this room. As Ashlee shook off the last vestiges of sleep, his legs trembled and his skin felt clammy against the cool air. The rest of the waking world filtered in, adding details and sensations he hadn't noticed before. Cars honked on the street below. Kids shouted as they rushed off to school. If not for the racket, Ashlee might have thought he was still deep inside Elden Ring. The waking reality was jarring, but the sudden understanding it brought was worth the shock. Ashlee nearly gasped as it came to him: the dream was more than a dream.

It was practice. It was training. It was the single greatest achievement of his gaming life.

Before another second passed, Ashlee planted himself in front of his high-end PC. His heart still pounded from the dream's urgency, and his entire body vibrated with anticipation. The only other time he had felt so alive was when he had beaten a particularly hard boss. It had taken all day and night to defeat that one, and the heady exhilaration had left him on an impossible high for days.

This was even better.

Adrenaline coursed through him, and his fingers moved with newfound precision. Ashlee's pulse quickened as he thought of his avatar, of the weight of armor, and of how deeply he had been inside it all. He had known the virtual space with more accuracy than he'd ever known his real-life surroundings. The movements and feelings lingered, as if his imagined self had transferred directly to the real world. In every conceivable way, Ashlee was still in that castle corridor.

He booted up Elden Ring, eager to see the results of his unexpected practice. Trembling hands moved with the speed and assurance of a man with a lifelong destiny. Ashlee immediately noticed that his actions were faster and more precise than ever before. Each flawless step showed the impact of his dream-training, and every seamless maneuver confirmed it. The dream's adrenaline fueled him through it all, and Ashlee lost himself in the mastery of his own movements.

It was as if his new skills were someone else's and he was just borrowing them. His hands flew over the controller with unexpected grace, translating subconscious muscle memory into perfect gameplay. It was an intoxicating, electrifying, unbelievable change, and Ashlee was powerless to resist. He wouldn't have wanted to, even if he could. The results were obvious. He couldn't wait to test them with friends.

He typed out a message, hardly pausing to consider what to say. The words flowed as easily as his flawless in-game movements. Ashlee didn't care that his friends were probably busy teaching or working or doing other, less important things. He didn't care that the clock showed an unreasonably early time for digital communication. He had to tell them. He had to share it.

His eagerness filled every pixel of the monitor and every letter of the text. "Guys, you won't believe it!" Ashlee wrote with as much intensity as the digital realm would allow. "I'm playing like a champion today!" His enthusiasm seeped from his fingertips onto the keyboard and into the crisp display of digital dialogue.

He could barely contain himself as he waited for his friends to see it. Tim and Ashley were usually quick to respond, and they always seemed as excited to game as he was. Ashlee grinned as he imagined what they'd say about his new, improved skills. He anticipated every response, savoring the build-up to the online session he was sure would happen. He knew he was ready for it. He was as ready as he'd ever be.

With each passing moment, the last of the dream slipped further away. The heaviness of imagined armor became the soft, comfortable weight of pajamas. His heartbeat began to settle, and the memory of stone corridors was slowly replaced by the reality of whitewashed walls. As Ashlee waited for his friends' reply, his mind wandered back to the castle.

He wished, just a little, that he was still in it.

Echoes of Transformation

At this hour, Ashlee expected his friends to be busy. Their prompt replies almost made him wonder if they'd been waiting for him. When the trio was online, Ashlee's transformation was obvious. Tim peppered the session with excited banter, saying, "What did you do? You're on fire today!" and Ashley punctuated his in-game prowess with bright, suspicious humor. Ashlee hardly noticed how his small apartment filled with keystrokes and chatter. He was too busy relishing the presence of friends who knew him so well. When the session briefly paused, he saw a silhouette near the doorway. Julia stood there, listening. The bright screen highlighted the concern on her face as his urgent, obsessive chatter worried her. Ashlee wondered how long she had been there, and she wondered how long this time would last.

In the two minutes it took for Ashlee's heart rate to return to normal, his friends had already replied to the message. Ashlee smiled with delight and disbelief. The only thing faster than his friends was his new set of skills. He knew Ashley was busy with online classes. He knew Tim was always juggling two or three new projects. At this time of day, he expected them to be distracted by students or lesson plans or the demands of real life. He almost believed they had been waiting for him.

Their eagerness confirmed Ashlee's hunch that this was going to be an epic session. The digital dialogue was practically shouting. "LET'S DO IT!" Tim had typed, showing his characteristic enthusiasm. "Bring on your A-game, Champion!" Ashley wrote with more exclamation marks than any one person should use in a lifetime. Ashlee felt the adrenaline return as the three of them launched into Elden Ring.

"Wow, you're on fire today!" Tim exclaimed as soon as they began. "Did you finally sacrifice a goat to the gaming gods or something?" Ashlee could hear the incredulous grin in Tim's voice. He could hear the keys clacking with excitement, too. Tim was known for his competitive streak, and Ashlee knew it must have been a shock for him to find someone else outpacing him.

Ashley wasn't any less surprised. Her voice rang with genuine joy as she peppered the session with cheerful banter. "Maybe he hired a professional to train him!" she laughed. "Did you download some special mods?" she teased. "Confess, Ashlee! How did you get so good?"

Ashlee hardly noticed how the sound of keystrokes and gaming chatter filled his small apartment. He was too busy relishing the presence of friends who knew him so well. Tim and Ashley's humor and energy made the digital space feel more like home than anything in the real world. Ashlee marveled at the technology that allowed him to connect with friends who were an ocean and several time zones away. The miracle of it didn't make him any less competitive, though. He showed off his improved skills with more than a little bit of pride.

His every move was smooth, confident, and perfect. There was no question that his dream-training had paid off. "Watch out!" Ashley called as Ashlee darted past a waiting enemy. His actions were seamless. "No fair!" Tim shouted as Ashlee's character effortlessly dodged another attack. "It's like the rest of us are standing still!"

In-game dialogue scrolled across Ashlee's screen as quickly as the real-time chatter that saturated the room. "How is this even possible?" Tim asked with playfully mock exasperation. "Are you even human anymore?" Ashley added with an imaginary gasp. "I think I might actually hate you!" said Tim, although his spirited voice made it clear that the truth was just the opposite.

The trio progressed further than they'd ever been. The fast-paced session filled the air with the sounds of shared triumph and lively keystrokes, charging the space with adrenaline and companionship. It was a comfort that only gamers knew. For Ashlee, it was like oxygen. He drew in huge, eager breaths of it, savoring the absolute freedom of his friends' virtual presence.

The ease of his movements showed in the efficiency of their progress. Before they knew it, the trio had reached the climax of a long, harrowing boss battle. Ashlee's fingers flew over the controller with unbelievable speed as Tim and Ashley shouted excited instructions. They hadn't seen a session like this in weeks. As the boss staggered and Tim whooped in celebration, the game paused for a brief cutscene. Ashlee stretched his arms over his head, relaxing for the first time since he'd woken.

That's when he saw her.

A silhouette hovered near the doorway. It was almost too dark to notice against the brightly lit screen, but when Ashlee looked closer, he knew exactly who it was. Julia's expression was unreadable as she stood and listened. Her face looked softer, more vulnerable, than usual. Ashlee wondered how long she'd been standing there.

When the screen faded back from the cutscene, her worry was impossible to miss. It cast long shadows across the room as the screen's glow threw everything into sharp relief. Julia was listening to the obsessive energy that saturated the apartment, and Ashlee knew that if he could hear it himself, it must have been worse for her. He wondered what she was thinking, then realized it was all too obvious.

There was a slight slump to her shoulders and a tightness to her jaw that showed exactly what was going through her mind. This time, her posture said, will be just like the last. Ashlee felt the stab of her worry before the boss battle resumed and Tim's excited shout filled the room again.

"Ashlee!" his friends called as his avatar took a hit. The urgency of the moment distracted him, but not enough. Julia's presence tugged at him even as his eyes stayed focused on the screen. She stood still and silent, a ghost in the doorway, while the sounds of clashing swords and rapid keystrokes reverberated through the space. Her presence was almost as intense as the gaming session itself, and Ashlee didn't know which would end first. He could hardly bear the thought of either.

An unexpected flurry of action pulled his focus back to the game. Ashlee winced at the tension in Julia's posture before she turned and walked away, her silhouette disappearing as quickly as it had come. As she left, the room's urgent energy crashed over him in full force, and Ashlee drowned in it.

A gleeful yelp escaped Tim as their enemy staggered again. "I can't believe it!" he shouted. "This is even more epic than last time!" Ashlee's attention drifted back to the game, back to his friends, and back to the excitement of the digital world.

Julia's concerns and her presence faded like echoes of echoes. Ashlee hardly noticed how empty the rest of the apartment felt without her in it.

Instead, he noticed the energy that hung in the air and the vivid colors that filled the screen. A moment later, the session was over. Ashlee and his friends had won. Ashlee and Julia had not.

As Tim and Ashley congratulated each other and made plans for another game soon, Ashlee stared at the door where Julia had been. He didn't know how long she'd stood there, and he didn't know how long this time would last. The tension lingered long after he said goodbye to his friends, setting the stage for more digital excitement, more real-world concern, and more conflicts he wasn't ready to face.

III

The Virtual Mentor

Whispers from the Sage

Ashlee lay cocooned in the clutter of his apartment, the gentle whirr of the computer serenading him to sleep. The room, a testament to his devotion to gaming, blurred around the edges until it transformed into a sprawling, surreal landscape. He stood in the midst of an Elden Ring dreamscape, clad in gritty armor that felt both foreign and familiar. A luminous pathway beckoned him toward a misty, ancient clearing, where an old figure named Eldred awaited with a knowing gaze. "You have a rare gift, Ashlee," Eldred intoned, breaking the fourth wall. "The ability to truly inhabit game worlds. But every gift carries risks and responsibilities." His voice echoed with the clang of distant battles and the rumble of thunderous roars. As Ashlee's hands tightened around the ethereal sword he wielded, his brow furrowed in a mixture of awe and sudden apprehension. The dream unfurled around him, vivid and inescapable.

The apartment was a sea of empty ramen cups and precarious towers of DVD cases. A disheveled bed, piled high with unwashed clothes, cradled Ashlee's sleeping form. The dim glow of the computer cast strange shadows, a comforting beacon in the chaos. For Ashlee, the clutter wasn't disorder; it was the tangible evidence of a life immersed in gaming, where every piece had its own story. The hum of the electronics melded with his breathing, forming a gentle lullaby that pulled him deeper into sleep.

As dreams began to weave their strange logic, the familiar contours of his room melted away. His bed elongated into a long, silvery path that shimmered with ethereal light, guiding him into a vast and fantastical expanse. Trees, impossibly tall and twisted, rose like sentinels from the mist. He felt the weight of the armor encasing him, both strange and yet an extension of himself, echoing his countless hours in virtual worlds.

Ashlee stood still, drinking in the strange wonder of the scene. He was no longer the slim thirty-year-old gamer with unkempt hair; here, he was a warrior in tarnished plate, gritty and majestic. The air crackled with energy, alive with the possibility of adventure and the shadow of unknown perils. Ashlee's hands, so used to the feel of a controller, gripped a sword that seemed to pulse with its own life force.

With tentative steps, he moved along the pathway. Every footfall reverberated with a metallic clang, echoing through the dreamlike landscape. Colors shifted in the mist, painting a constantly changing backdrop of eerie beauty. Somewhere beyond the horizon, thunder growled like a distant beast. This was not just a dream; it was a realm that teetered on the edge of reality, drawing him further into its depths.

The luminous trail wound through tangled forests and over desolate hills, leading him toward a clearing that glowed with ancient mystery. His pulse quickened with a blend of exhilaration and uncertainty. Here, the world felt endless, unbounded by the limits of code or imagination. It was a place where anything might happen, and where he was more alive than ever.

At last, he reached the clearing, and there, in the midst of its ghostly light, stood Eldred. The figure was as timeless as the landscape itself, wrapped in robes that whispered of long-forgotten epochs. A beard like spun silver framed his face, and eyes, deep with knowledge, met Ashlee's with a gaze that pierced the soul. Eldred exuded an aura of serene omnipotence, a sage who had seen ages come and go.

"You have a rare gift, Ashlee," Eldred's voice resonated, seeming to speak not only to Ashlee but to the very fabric of the dream. "The ability to truly inhabit game worlds." His words were measured, each one falling like a stone in a pond, sending ripples through the surreal expanse. "But every gift carries risks and responsibilities."

The proclamation hung in the air, profound and heavy with meaning. Ashlee's mind raced to grasp the full weight of it. Was this just a dream, or was it something more? A message from the universe, or from his own restless subconscious? The possibilities swirled, luminous and enticing.

All around them, the surreal world shifted and sighed. The clang of weapons and distant roars of mythical creatures underscored Eldred's words, a symphony of the fantastical. The ground trembled underfoot as if the very earth pulsed with anticipation. Every sense was alive, attuned to the strangeness of the moment.

Ashlee tightened his grip on the ethereal sword. This was his realm, his sanctuary, yet it had never felt so real—or so fraught with potential peril. What did Eldred mean by risks and responsibilities? The question burned in him, an ember that refused to die. He was both enthralled and apprehensive, caught in a web of excitement and dread.

The dream, with its surreal clarity, wrapped around him like a cloak. Ashlee's thoughts churned, a tempest of wonder and worry. Here, in this fantastical space, he stood on the precipice of something vast and unknown. The echo of Eldred's words lingered, a haunting refrain in a landscape teeming with mystery. And as the dream unfurled, Ashlee found himself lost in its vivid and inescapable embrace.

Lessons Between Worlds

Ashlee sat at the lectern, barely awake in the modest classroom where he'd taught the same lesson too many times. His eyelids drooped like the eager students' attention spans, which strayed from their notebooks to the more alluring glow of their phones. Chen Laoshi, poised and perceptive at the front, noticed his glazed expression. "Perhaps we might consider a different approach today, Ashlee," she suggested, her voice both gentle and amused. He shifted in his chair, fingers trembling as they fumbled with the lesson plan. The hum of the projector and the murmur of students accentuated his struggle to bridge the gap between the echo of his dream and the reality of his responsibilities.

The classroom was a small but lively space, walls adorned with bright posters about international culture. The morning sun streamed through half-closed blinds, painting slanted patterns on rows of well-used desks. The air buzzed with youthful energy, yet beneath it was a quiet tension, as students half-heartedly doodled or furtively tapped on their phones. Ashlee could sense their waning interest, a mirror to his own preoccupied state.

He sat hunched over the lectern, his posture echoing countless late nights bent over a console. The vision from his sleep clung to him like a ghost, leaving him both thrilled and deeply distracted. In his mind, Eldred's voice still reverberated: "You have a rare gift, Ashlee." What did it mean? How could he think about teaching when all he wanted was to explore the depths of that dream world?

Chen Laoshi stood near the whiteboard, her presence crisp and composed. Her eyes swept the room before landing back on Ashlee. Even from across the space, she seemed to sense his turmoil. With deliberate steps, she approached, her heels tapping softly on the tiled floor.

"Ashlee," she said in a gentle, amused tone. "Perhaps we might consider a different approach today."

Her words cut through the fog in his mind. He glanced up, offering a sheepish smile that barely reached his eyes. "Yeah, uh, maybe a more interactive session," he mumbled, still caught between the two worlds.

Chen nodded, her expression both understanding and mildly concerned. "It seems our students are not the only ones a bit unengaged today," she observed, the hint of a smile playing at her lips.

Ashlee tried to refocus, shifting his weight as he looked at the lesson plan before him. But the words swam on the page, interspersed with the more urgent call of his night-time vision. Digital media was supposed to be his forte, yet now the phrases seemed hollow, dwarfed by the grandeur of the dream that had captured his imagination.

The projector hummed softly, its light a stark contrast to the vibrant glow of his subconscious. Students whispered, trading notes or simply succumbing to the lure of social media. The classroom felt distant and removed, like a world he no longer belonged to.

"Um, what do you think about breaking into groups?" he suggested, attempting to regain a semblance of authority. "Discuss how media influences, uh, daily life." His voice faltered as he finished, lacking the confidence that usually accompanied his teaching.

A few students perked up at the idea of a change in routine, while others continued to tune out, eyes glued to tiny screens. Ashlee's fingers trembled on the lectern, their dexterity wasted on this task. He glanced at Chen, who watched him with an empathetic gaze.

"Sometimes, it's hard to focus on reality when our minds are elsewhere," she offered, her words filled with quiet insight.

Ashlee nodded, a small huff of laughter escaping his lips. "You have no idea," he replied, though he suspected she might. His thoughts wandered back to Eldred and the surreal landscape, longing pulling at him like a magnetic force.

With a deep breath, he tried to immerse himself in the classroom again. "All right," he called out, his voice barely cutting through the low chatter. "Let's, uh, hear some thoughts on digital life and reality."

He walked between the desks, listening to the snippets of conversation. Most of it was off-topic, though he caught glimpses of engagement here and there. Still, the dream lingered at the edge of his consciousness, its allure more compelling than any lesson he might deliver.

As the minutes ticked by, he attempted to bring his focus back, but every action felt hollow. The gulf between his dream and this duty grew more pronounced, the line between fantasy and reality blurred. He wondered if he could ever bridge it, if the two worlds could coexist without one consuming the other.

The bell finally rang, a merciful release from his internal struggle. Students filed out, their faces alight with relief and chatter. Ashlee remained behind, sinking into a chair as he tried to quiet the echoes of Eldred's message.

Chen lingered too, offering a reassuring nod as she gathered her things. "Sometimes the heart is pulled in more than one direction," she said simply, before leaving him alone with his thoughts.

The classroom emptied, its echoes mingling with Ashlee's own, the morning leaving him adrift between the pull of responsibility and the desire to return to a world where his passions truly thrived.

Chasing the Elusive Guide

That evening, Ashlee returned to his console, the dim glow of his apartment enveloping him like a cocoon as he sought to reconnect with the dream world. His fingers danced over the buttons, guiding him through Elden Ring with the precision of a veteran gamer. He scanned every familiar alcove, hoping for a profound dialogue with Eldred. Instead, he found the standard NPC chatter that barely registered beyond routine mechanical greetings. He sat momentarily still, pressing the controller with a slight frown and exhaling in frustration. The gentle clack of keys and the ensuing silence between in-game actions set the stage for his growing uncertainty. "Eldred?" he repeated softly into the empty digital air, the absence of his mentor's voice deepening the rift between his two worlds.

The apartment was a sanctuary of soft light and quiet determination. After a day filled with restless thoughts, Ashlee found solace in the flickering screen before him. It was here, in this dimly lit world, that he felt most himself, most at ease. The contrast between his earlier distraction and his current focus was palpable, every ounce of his attention locked onto the console as he prepared to dive back into the realm that haunted his dreams.

His fingers moved with expert precision, navigating menus and selecting gear with the fluidity of a seasoned player. Excitement bubbled beneath the surface, a quiet anticipation that perhaps tonight would bring another encounter with the enigmatic Eldred. The dream had been so vivid, so real—surely it was more than a mere flight of fancy. As the game's opening scenes played out, he felt a rush of possibility and hope.

Ashlee's avatar emerged in the game world, armor gleaming under a virtual sun. The digital landscape unfolded with familiar beauty, yet every corner seemed to promise something new. He set out with determined intent, retracing the steps he had taken in his dream, convinced that Eldred's presence awaited him somewhere within the game's sprawling expanse.

He journeyed through shadowy forests and open plains, scanning each alcove and ruin for a sign of the ancient figure. His heart quickened with each turn, convinced that the encounter was just around the next corner. But as the minutes stretched on, anticipation gave way to a creeping doubt.

Non-player characters, or NPCs, dotted the landscape, each one delivering their pre-scripted lines with mechanical precision. "Well met, traveler," one greeted, words as empty and repetitive as Ashlee's unanswered questions. "May your blade stay sharp," another intoned, as Ashlee sped past with barely a glance. These interactions were routine, predictable, nothing like the profound and personal dialogue he'd experienced in the dream.

Frustration edged into his movements. He doubled back, revisiting places where he'd felt Eldred's presence most strongly. Again, there were only the same standard greetings, the same hollow words. It was as if the dream had sealed itself away, refusing to be captured or recreated in the waking world.

The apartment's dim light wrapped around him like a soft, isolating blanket. The coziness that once comforted now seemed to press in on him, underscoring the solitude of his search. His earlier distraction was nothing compared to the uncertainty that gnawed at him now, each unanswered question widening the chasm between his two worlds.

Ashlee's fingers slowed on the controller, their dance less certain, more resigned. The soft clack of buttons echoed in the room, a stark contrast to the vibrant game music that usually filled his evenings. Even the digital landscape seemed to grow quieter, as if sensing his growing disillusionment.

He paused the game, taking a moment to collect himself. Maybe he'd been foolish to think that the dream could be recaptured so easily. Maybe it had been nothing more than his imagination playing tricks. But the encounter had felt so real, Eldred's words so urgent. He couldn't let it go, not yet.

With renewed determination, he resumed his search. But each new attempt met with the same impersonal chatter, the same silence where he longed for connection. Ashlee's shoulders sagged slightly, a physical manifestation of the disappointment settling over him like a mist.

His voice was a whisper, tentative and filled with longing. "Eldred?" he called into the empty digital expanse, half expecting the figure to materialize from thin air. But the only response was the quiet hum of the console and the scripted NPC lines, repeating themselves with mechanical fidelity.

Ashlee leaned back, exhaling slowly. The weight of the dream—and its absence—pressed down on him. He had crossed the threshold between fantasy and reality, only to find himself stranded between them, unsure which side he truly belonged to.

The room was silent except for the ambient sounds of the game, a stark contrast to the vibrant noise of his imagination. Here, in the muted glow, Ashlee confronted the void left by the dream's elusive promise. It was a silence that spoke volumes, amplifying the tension between his desires and the world as it was.

Yet even as the night's search drew to a close, a spark of hope remained. The dream had come to him once; it could come again. The rift between his worlds might yet be bridged, if only he could find the path back to it. With that thought lingering like a faint beacon, he pressed the controller once more, his determination as relentless as the longing that fueled it.

IV
Reality Blurs

When the Game Invades Reality

Ashlee wandered the quiet grocery aisle, where the fluorescent lights hummed and cast a sterile glow over towers of boxed noodles. He reached for a can of soup when the world suddenly became a frenzied, screaming swirl of impossible colors. It was Mario Kart 8, and he was in it. A wheel in his hands, he sped through the world with terror in his eyes, colors sharp and bold around him as a sweet tang of cartoon madness filled his nose. He swerved, losing breath and gaining panic, the engine's roar drowning his thoughts. Then reality snapped back like an elastic band, leaving him in a heap in the center of the store. Shoppers stared as if he'd grown another head. Wei Lin rushed over, her voice cutting through the surreal haze like a clear, bright bell. Ashlee tried to speak, but only managed a few syllables before he fled, eyes wide and heart still pounding like a drum in his chest.

He staggered to the exit, his mind barely registering the familiar beep of the automatic door. Outside, the world was blessedly still. No flying blue shells or trickster bananas in sight. Just the usual crowd, as ordinary as milk, flowing around him like he was an island in a river of bored humanity. But he couldn't breathe. Each inhale stuck in his throat like peanut butter. The pavement swayed under his feet, a sudden drop of vertigo turning his knees to jelly. Clutching a metal cart corral, Ashlee fumbled his way to the edge of the parking lot. He leaned against a streetlight, willing his pulse to slow down, feeling like a cracked character in someone else's reality show.

"Dude. What the hell just happened?" The words whispered past him on the lips of a bored-looking teen as Ashlee slid along the sidewalk, his escape clumsy and desperate. The bright, boxy letters of the grocery store's sign blinked at him, each flash a little too loud. He gulped the humid afternoon air as if he'd just broken the surface of a lake, his breath gradually finding its rhythm again. Finally, when he thought he could stand without falling apart, Ashlee headed home. But even the mundane rumble of traffic seemed surreal, a strange, ironic soundtrack to his half-stunned retreat.

After the Glitch: A Moment of Clarity

Ashlee stumbled into their apartment, the door swinging shut with a bang that echoed his rattled nerves. Julia was in the living room, mid-sweep with the vacuum cleaner's soft hum undercutting his jagged breathing. He looked like a man on the run, hair wild and face pale. Dropping onto the sofa, he spilled his story like a shaken can of soda. Words flew out, bubbling over with frantic detail: the grocery aisle, the sudden kaleidoscope of a cartoon track, the wheel, the colors, the panic that felt so real. Julia stopped, a statue in mid-tidy, her eyes locking onto his with a mix of skepticism and deepening concern. When he paused to breathe, she moved next to him, her touch grounding him as she said, "This is serious. I think you should see someone." The words landed between them like a jolt, electric and unsettling. He managed a weak smile, but the fear lingered, a ghost that wouldn't let go.

"Julia, it was insane," Ashlee continued, the last echoes of his laughter catching in his throat. He looked at her, his eyes wide and pleading. The comfort of the room, with its soft lighting and familiar clutter, seemed a universe away from the chaos still buzzing in his mind. His heart was a wild animal in his chest, refusing to calm. "I was just picking up groceries, and then bam! I was in the game. Like, actually in it."

She watched him, her expression shifting from disbelief to a careful, deliberate patience. "Slow down, Ash. You're not making sense," she said, choosing each word with the precision of someone assembling a fragile puzzle.

Ashlee raked a hand through his hair, the action as desperate as his tone. "I don't even know how to explain it. I was standing there, looking at cans, and then I'm in a kart. The colors, the sounds—everything was so intense. I thought I was going to crash. And then, suddenly, I'm back in the store, and everyone's looking at me like I'm crazy."

Julia moved closer, sitting down next to him. Her presence was a steady force, pulling him back from the edge of his panic. "And then what happened?" she asked, the words gentle, as if coaxing a frightened animal out of hiding.

"I just... I couldn't take it. I left." His voice was a whisper now, the frenzy collapsing into exhaustion. "I don't know what's happening to me, Jules." The confession hung in the air, raw and vulnerable.

Julia let the silence stretch, feeling its weight. She held his gaze, her own eyes filled with a mix of tenderness and something else, something more like fear than she'd ever allow him to see. "Ashlee," she began, her voice as firm as her grip on his shoulder, "I think this is serious. Maybe you need to talk to someone, a professional."

He flinched at the suggestion, pulling away slightly. "I'm not losing it," he insisted, his voice catching on the edge of defiance.

"No one's saying that." Her tone softened, brushing against his frayed nerves like a calming hand. "But this isn't normal, Ash. You need to figure out what's going on."

He looked around the room, at the pile of magazines, the half-folded laundry, the normalcy he couldn't quite reach. "What if it happens again?" he asked, the question small, like a child's.

"We'll handle it," Julia replied, the certainty in her voice a lifeline he couldn't yet grasp. She gave him a look that was all warmth and worry, an unspoken promise lingering between them.

Ashlee drew a shaky breath, the weight of her words settling into his bones. "I just... I didn't think it was this bad," he admitted, his eyes not meeting hers.

She wrapped an arm around him, pulling him closer. "It's going to be okay. But you have to be honest about it. With me and with yourself." The conviction in her voice was unyielding, a beacon in the confusion.

Ashlee managed a smile, a faint, tremulous curve of his lips. "Yeah, I guess 'Help, I'm in a video game' isn't your typical issue," he said, his attempt at humor thin but sincere.

Julia returned his smile, her eyes holding the depths of her concern. "No, it's not," she replied, her words edged with a soft, knowing amusement.

They sat together in the dim room, the closeness easing some of the fear's sharp edges. Ashlee leaned into her, feeling the exhaustion finally overtaking him. The sound of the city outside was distant, a lullaby of honking horns and muffled voices. It wrapped around them as the last bits of adrenaline seeped away, leaving Ashlee drained but anchored.

"Thanks, Julia," he said, closing his eyes as if to shut out the lingering specters of his experience. Her embrace was the only thing holding him in place, a thread of sanity in a world turned strange.

"Anytime," she whispered, resting her head against his. The moment stretched, their breaths finding a shared rhythm, the room enveloping them in its warmth. The threat of Ashlee's earlier panic receded into the quiet, but it hovered still, an uneasy guest in their cozy world. He held onto her, half-expecting the real world to vanish again. But it didn't. For now, the only tracks were the ones they left on the cushions as they sank further into each other, waiting together for whatever might come next.

V

The Gaming Circle

Arena of Camaraderie

Neon light pulsed in rhythm with the music as Ashlee's slender fingers tapped rapidly at the controller, his eyes focused on the chaotic battle raging onscreen. Across the room, Tim arrived with a duffel bag and a competitive gleam in his eye, throwing a casual wave to the blur of red hair that signaled Ashley's presence in the online chat.

"Guess who's back?" Tim shouted, dropping onto the couch and instantly syncing into the match. Laughter erupted as pixels exploded in bursts of color, the apartment alive with sound and banter. Marcus, aka KnightSlayer92, made his debut with a crisp message: "Thought I'd stop by and see what all the fuss is about. xD" The apartment filled with the clack of controllers and the glow of screens, an arena for Ashlee's unmatched skills.

"You must be cheating, Ashlee!" Tim shouted with a teasing grin, watching his character soar helplessly off the map. Ashley laughed into her headset, wide-eyed with admiration.

"I can't believe how good you've gotten!" she marveled, and Marcus leaned forward, clearly impressed.

"Ever thought of joining my Elden Ring clan?" he typed, as Julia watched from the side, her eyes shifting from the screen to Ashlee with a mix of quiet amusement and growing concern.

Bright light from the TV flickered over Ashlee's face as he leaned in, fully absorbed. Tim threw his jacket over a chair and pulled out a controller, syncing up without missing a beat.

"Already in the lead? Typical!" Tim laughed, joining the chaos onscreen.

Ashlee flashed a quick smile, his focus still locked. "Better catch up," he said. "You know I don't hold back."

A loud explosion erupted from the game, and Tim's character flew across the screen. "Ouch! Brutal, dude!" Tim exclaimed, his fingers jamming at the buttons.

Ashley's voice came through clearly, bubbly with excitement. "And here I thought I'd have time to warm up!" she chimed in, her character diving into the fray with renewed energy.

"More like getting smoked!" Tim retorted, winking at Ashlee as he settled deeper into the couch. His eyes darted around the room, catching sight of a brightly decorated corner filled with game cases and figurines. The living room had been transformed into a gamer's paradise, screens blinking like an electronic jungle.

Marcus's message appeared again, this time with a friendly jab: "Hope you don't mind me crashing the party. :P" He joined the match, his character taking shape onscreen with practiced flair.

"Glad you made it, Marcus," Ashlee called out, giving a thumbs-up toward the screen. His American accent mingled with gaming lingo, a familiar harmony to the group.

"Don't think I'll go easy on you," Marcus replied, his avatar swinging a massive sword. "Ready for some competition!"

They dove back into the game, the room an energetic hub of sound and movement. Buttons clacked like a fast-paced percussion, and the game's music blared in sync with their enthusiasm. Ashley's voice was a constant thread, laughing and cheering as she fought to keep pace.

"This is wild!" she shouted. "How are you pulling these moves, Ashlee?"

"Wouldn't you like to know?" Ashlee teased, dodging another onscreen attack with incredible precision. His skills were undeniable, and the room was alive with playful accusations.

Tim waved his arms dramatically as his character went flying again. "Stop ganging up on me!" he yelled, his glasses slipping down his nose. "Ashley, help a guy out!"

"Can't do much when you're running off the map," Ashley shot back with a giggle, her character barely hanging on in the fast-paced battle.

Ashlee laughed, his concentration unwavering. "Need some extra lives, Tim?" he joked, deftly avoiding another onscreen explosion.

Julia stood nearby, arms crossed but smiling at the chaos. Her gaze shifted between the screen and Ashlee, catching his passion and the camaraderie he shared with his friends. The gaming session was an arena of virtual competition, yet it highlighted something deeper—the connection and joy Ashlee found in these moments.

Marcus typed quickly, adding to the friendly rivalry. "You've been practicing!" he noted, surprised by Ashlee's dominance in the game. "My clan would love you, haha."

The matches continued, a whirl of digital action and lively exchanges. Tim's gestures grew more animated with each round, feigning disbelief at Ashlee's unrelenting performance. "Seriously, man, you've leveled up!" he exclaimed, shaking his head with a grin.

"I might have found a new game to master," Ashlee replied, his tone both humble and excited. His character triumphed again, adding to his victory streak.

Lights from the screens painted the walls in a shifting dance of colors, casting everyone in vibrant hues. Ashley's enthusiasm came through clearly, a constant reminder of the shared fun. "Marcus, I didn't know you played anything besides Elden Ring!" she teased, her voice laced with warmth.

"Branching out!" Marcus responded. "And glad I did. This is a blast."

"You guys are making me look bad," Tim groaned, still focused but clearly enjoying the friendly competition. "I need to log more hours!"

"Bring it, Tim!" Ashlee taunted, relishing the challenge. "Or maybe I'll start playing Elden Ring."

"Then I'm in trouble!" Marcus typed, full of camaraderie. "Join me any time!"

Julia watched the exchanges, her smile tinged with thoughtfulness. Ashlee's eyes sparkled with the thrill of the game, the virtual worlds where he seemed to belong most. Her expression shifted as she observed him, from light amusement to something deeper—a concern that lingered beneath the surface.

The session stretched on, filled with laughter and mock protest as Tim, Ashley, and Marcus rallied against Ashlee's dominance. The air buzzed with energy, the kind that only came from being fully immersed and surrounded by friends. Julia's presence was a subtle counterpoint, a reminder of the world beyond the screens.

"I think I've found my new rival!" Marcus announced, clearly impressed by Ashlee's skills. "Great playing with you all!"

Ashley cheered into the headset, her spirit undampened. "So fun, guys! Let's do this again soon!"

Tim set his controller down with a dramatic sigh. "Ashlee, I don't know how you do it," he said, playfully defeated but happy. "Guess I'll have to visit more often."

Ashlee grinned, his face flushed with excitement. "Anytime, Tim. You know you're welcome."

They laughed together, the apartment resonating with the kind of joy that only came from shared experiences. But as the noise settled, Julia's quiet concern lingered, a shadow beneath the bright lights.

Bridging the Divide

Ashlee leaned back against the sofa, his fingers still buzzing from the night's digital warfare, as the last sounds of laughter faded into the hallway. The apartment, moments ago alive with vibrant color and noise, now lay in the quiet, reflective hum of cooling consoles and scattered game cases. Julia watched him, her face partially shadowed in the soft light. She took a slow breath, then spoke with gentle precision.

"I'm afraid I'm losing you to these virtual worlds, Ashlee." Her words hung in the air, heavy and delicate as she uncrossed her arms and reached for him.

He hesitated, caught between exhilaration and unease. "You know it's not like that," he replied, though a flicker of doubt betrayed him. He leaned forward, taking her hand, his earnest expression showing both passion and worry.

The contrast between the night's exuberance and this intimate moment wrapped around them, a silent acknowledgment of what lay unspoken but keenly felt.

The apartment was dim now, with only the soft glow of the TV casting long shadows across the room. Game cases and controllers lay strewn around like remnants of a storm, a vivid reminder of the night's intensity. Julia's eyes took it all in, lingering on Ashlee's flushed cheeks and the subtle twitch in his fingers.

"I just," she paused, choosing her words carefully. "I just want to make sure we're not drifting apart."

Ashlee squeezed her hand, his voice a blend of sincerity and defensiveness. "I'm here, Julia. Really."

"You're here, but you're not here," she countered softly, her gaze unflinching. The residual hum of the gaming rig underscored the silence that followed, a tangible presence in the room.

He looked down, trying to bridge the gap between their worlds. "It's just... It's what I love to do. You know that."

Her eyes softened, but her resolve remained. "I do know," she admitted. "But I also know how easy it is for you to get lost in it."

His mind flashed to the battles, the laughter, the sense of achievement. "You saw how much fun we had," he said, almost pleadingly. "It's not just games; it's connection. It's..."

"Everything to you," she finished, her voice laced with both understanding and worry.

Ashlee bit his lip, caught between passion and guilt. "I want it to work, Julia. All of it."

She leaned in closer, her expression a mixture of determination and affection. "Then we have to find balance, Ashlee. We have to try."

His heart raced with the echoes of the night's excitement, but he nodded, feeling the weight of her words settle. "I will. I promise," he said, though the uncertainty lingered between them.

The room seemed larger now, the space between them both physical and emotional. Ashlee's eyes darted to the TV, where the game menu still flickered, then back to Julia's searching face. Her presence was a grounding force, a tether to the real world that sometimes felt just out of reach.

"We're in this together, right?" he asked, his voice barely above a whisper.

She smiled softly, a glimmer of hope shining through. "I want to be," she said, resting her head on his shoulder. "I really do."

The air felt heavy with the promise of change, but the love and tension wove a fragile understanding. Julia's patience and Ashlee's desire to meet her halfway hung delicately in the balance, capturing the essence of their unspoken fears and dreams.

They sat like that, close yet distant, surrounded by the traces of Ashlee's virtual escapades. The silence filled with meaning, punctuated by the gentle rhythm of their breaths and the quiet murmur of the city beyond. For now, the conversation had paused, but the sense of what lay ahead was clear.

"We can make this work, can't we?" Ashlee ventured, his tone both hopeful and uncertain.

Julia didn't answer right away. Instead, she nestled closer, her warmth a silent reassurance. "We can try," she finally replied, holding him tighter as if anchoring them both to a shared reality.

Her insistence on finding balance resonated in the dim light, a beacon of both challenge and commitment. Ashlee closed his eyes, nodding again with conflicted resolve. This time, the words felt different—a starting point, a promise.

As the night wore on, the glow of the gaming setup dimmed, leaving them in the gentle light of something not yet defined but deeply felt. The world outside continued its distant hum, but inside, a new focus emerged, fragile and waiting to be claimed.

VI

The Digital Landscape

The first splash of movement found Ashlee leaping across brightly colored platforms, where his steps echoed like soft explosions of pixels and the air fizzed with retro, eight-bit excitement. Suddenly, the dream bled into a dust-choked ruin, crumbling towers rising like broken teeth around him as he sprinted through the gritty landscape, every breath a tang of rust and decay. Before his mind could adjust, a sudden heaviness clamped down, and he was struggling through deep water, every kick of his legs slow and muted. Even in the pressure and murk, he recognized the parade of characters as he sped past—plumber, survivor, aquatic guide—all tipping their hats with amused familiarity.

The landscape lurched, bouncing him back into the playful, primary-colored world of Super Mario. He ran, fueled by an absurd energy, past soft, rounded hills and platforms that floated impossibly in midair. Coins spun lazily above him, and the blue sky grinned with oversized clouds. The soles of his shoes met every pixelated surface with a gentle thunk, like an oversized kid's drumset. Cheerful sound effects chased his progress, a rapid-fire chorus of beeps and boings, and the digital world shimmered as if alive. As he moved, the air was a sweet and charged, humming with nostalgia and the crackling thrill of retro possibility.

Just as his lungs seemed to catch up with the pace, the dreamworld flickered, plunging him into the gritty realism of a post-apocalyptic nightmare. The once vibrant palette became ash and dirt, muted grays and browns stretching to a horizon stained with industrial blight. The oppressive quiet pressed in, broken only by the crunch of debris under his feet. Polluted air filled his lungs, a rough texture of dust and sand, and the taste of irradiated water cut sharp on his tongue. Ashlee's pace quickened, and even as the weight of the landscape pressed down, his feet seemed to know the way, following the ruined streets and concrete scars.

In this barren world, a character appeared, cutting an absurd contrast. The animated plumber himself, wide-eyed and pixel-perfect, grinned from beneath his iconic red cap. With a knowing wink and a jaunty salute, he called out to Ashlee, "You're a long way from the Mushroom Kingdom, eh?" before springing away with an exaggerated bounce. Ashlee laughed, a sound swallowed by the ruins, but even In the harsh landscape, the absurdity and warmth of the interaction brought a lightness to his step.

Suddenly, the scenery warped once more, jolting him back to the brightly colored, soft-focus world of the Mario-like setting. It was a joyful chaos of moving platforms and spinning coins, an orchestrated explosion of color and sound. Every movement was buoyant, lifting him effortlessly over obstacles that should have seemed impossible. He breathed in the crisp, clean sensation of this imagined space, almost tasting the sweet data that filled it. The very fabric of the world pulsed with a rhythmic simplicity that made each leap a perfectly timed beat, part of a bizarre but satisfying dance.

But no sooner had he found the rhythm than the dream twisted again, the color bleeding into the stark, choking atmosphere of the Fallout-inspired realm. This time, the oppressive feeling seemed to claw at him, the air so thick with dust and despair that it almost felt solid. His footsteps were heavy, and every breath carried the grit of a thousand lost stories. The earth felt unstable beneath him, each crumbling concrete slab and twisted metal girder a reminder of the futility that pervaded this space. But Ashlee kept moving, driven by an urgency he didn't fully understand.

A new character emerged, hauntingly human in this abandoned world. A ragged survivor, hollow-eyed and shadowed, nodded to Ashlee with a grim familiarity. "Welcome to the wasteland," he murmured, his voice like wind over broken glass. Though his expression was tired, there was a hint of respect, even camaraderie, as he gestured Ashlee onward. The interaction lent a surreal depth to the dream, the weight of connection amid the emptiness. Ashlee recognized himself in the figure's solitary stance, and he ran with renewed determination, a shared understanding propelling him through the crumbling cityscape.

With a dizzying shift, the dream submerged him into the deep ocean world of Subnautica. The water pressed against him with a heavy insistence, every movement slow and muted as he pushed through the dim, liquid expanse. Blue light filtered down in ghostly shafts, illuminating the alien life that floated around him. Bubbles escaped from his mouth, tiny balloons that trailed his path like forgotten thoughts. He felt the pressure on his skin and in his ears, the sensation both disconcerting and comforting, like an embrace from another world. Even sound was strange here, a muted echo of reality that reached him only after it had been stretched and altered by the depths.

In the murk, a figure appeared—graceful and fluid, part of the sea itself. The aquatic guide, fins shimmering like stars in the abyss, extended a webbed hand toward Ashlee. "Follow me," the words were soft, like bubbles breaking the surface, and her eyes were wise with the secrets of the deep. There was an uncanny familiarity to her presence, as if she were not just a guide in this ocean but through the dream itself. Her presence added an otherworldly sense of direction, urging him on through the dark and the strange. Ashlee reached toward her, fingers brushing water and light.

Without warning, he was above water again, thrust back into the vibrant chaos of the Mario-like realm. The world around him was a blur of impossible geometry, a frenzy of motion that somehow made perfect sense. The playful abandon of it filled him with an exhilaration that was nearly tangible, every bounce and leap a thrill that buzzed in his very bones. He moved with an effortless precision, the surreal logic of the space bending to his will. It was a child's dream, unrestrained and joyous, and he embraced the wild logic as he dashed across the imaginary terrain.

Then, a final jarring transition hurled him into the dust and decay once more. The Fallout landscape stretched endlessly, its hopelessness a sharp contrast to the whimsy from which he'd come. But this time, there was a clarity in his sprint, a single-mindedness that pushed him past the crumbling reminders of civilization lost. He breathed in the heavy, particulate-laden air, each lungful a testament to the endurance of both body and dream. Ashlee ran, the characters and worlds a chaotic blur, familiar yet distant, and as he sped through the haunting landscape, everything seemed to stretch and slow and press in around him until it all but shattered.

Resurfacing with Scars

Ashlee awoke to a dim room and a body slick with sweat, limbs shaking from the intensity of the dreamworld he'd just left. The familiar clutter of his apartment, once comforting in its disarray, felt strangely muted and foreign. Posters of gaming worlds he'd traversed a hundred times watched him from the walls with indifferent stares, and the low hum of his computer filled the room with a sound that now seemed far too mundane. He lay there for a moment, letting reality creep back in as his breathing slowed, the vivid chaos of the night leaving behind a shadow of discontent.

With effort, he swung his legs off the bed and into the cold embrace of another Beijing morning. A few quick swipes of his hair made it slightly less wild, and he rubbed his eyes as if trying to wipe away the dream residue. As he moved through the apartment, everything seemed to hold less color and less sound, a bleak imitation of what his mind had just spun together. His fingers, nimble on a controller, fumbled with the coffee machine. His phone chimed with messages he wasn't ready to read, demands from a world that felt one-dimensional and dull. He stared at his breakfast, half-eaten cereal gone soggy in the bowl, his thoughts drifting back to the pixelated skies and haunted ruins of the night before.

By the time he reached the international school, the day had slipped into a grey routine. He drifted through the familiar halls like a ghost, passing colorful bulletin boards and lively student projects that felt far too real for him to connect with. In the classroom, he settled into his chair with a posture that spoke of long hours at the screen rather than dedication to teaching. The whiteboard waited, blank and expectant, but Ashlee's mind was elsewhere.

Standing before his students, he attempted an explanation that even he barely understood. "So, the next step is..." He paused, blinking at the words he'd started to write. "...right." The students exchanged glances, their eyes questioning but not unkind. They'd seen him like this before, a teacher who sometimes wandered through lessons like a dreamer searching for an exit. Today, his distraction seemed more pronounced, more dissonant.

He continued, his words as scattered as his thoughts. "Um, any questions so far?" His gaze slid over the room, not really settling on any one student. The silence stretched, awkward and telling, before one brave soul raised a hand. "Mr. Montgomery, is everything okay?" Ashlee nodded, perhaps too eagerly, a smile flashing then fading. "Yeah, totally fine. Just, uh, running on low hit points today." A few of them laughed, more out of politeness than understanding. The metaphor hung there, incomplete and sad, much like Ashlee's presence in the room.

The class crawled along, and he fought to keep the thread from slipping away entirely. "Remember, when you're solving this, it's like..." Another pause, longer this time. "...solving a puzzle in reverse." It wasn't the most coherent analogy, but it had enough pieces to work with, and some of the students began scribbling notes again. Ashlee's eyes drifted toward the window, where the grey sky mirrored the washed-out hues of his day.

When the bell finally announced the end of the lesson, the students filed out with looks that mixed curiosity and concern. Ashlee's gaze lingered on the door, following them as if their exit left the room significantly emptier. A few hung back, asking questions with hesitance that revealed their true intent: "Are you really okay?" "Is the homework due tomorrow?" "Did we do something wrong?" He assured them, each response more distracted than the last. "I'm fine." "It's due next week." "You're doing great."

The brief reprieve between classes was spent nursing a cooling cup of coffee, the taste bitter and real. He moved to the teachers' lounge, where the room was filled with low chatter and the smell of reheated lunches. Even here, among colleagues, his thoughts remained a million miles away—or perhaps just a few pixels off.

"Hey, Ashlee." A friendly voice pulled him back for a moment. "You seem a little out of it today." He turned to the speaker, a fellow expat with a knowing grin. "Late night grinding?" Ashlee chuckled, the sound more reflex than genuine. "Something like that." He stirred the coffee absentmindedly, spilling a few drops without noticing. "Or just trying to farm enough sleep for once."

The conversation continued without him, snippets of it reaching his ears while his mind wandered. "...curriculum changes..." "...upcoming parent-teacher conference..." Each topic found little purchase, the words floating past like debris in his chaotic dream world. His hands toyed with the edges of a worksheet, eyes staring through it. His coworkers shared looks, a silent acknowledgment of his state, before returning to their own matters.

Even as the day wore on, his ability to focus seemed to dwindle rather than recover. He returned to the classroom for the last lessons, each minute dragging into the next like an endless tutorial level. More than once, he lost his place in the middle of a sentence, backtracking over both his thoughts and his written words. A few students asked if they were covering the right material. A few more asked if he'd gone AFK.

As the final bell of the day sounded, Ashlee gathered his things with a slow, deliberate pace. The exhaustion of the real world weighed heavily on him, but beneath it, a restless energy waited, eager to return to the night's vivid escapes. The hallway was filled with the noise of students ready to face the world, bright and real and full of their own adventures. He moved through them, parting the crowd like a specter, invisible in his own right.

By the time he reached the doors of the school, the grey sky had darkened, and the wind carried the chill of a November evening. Ashlee paused at the threshold, the reality of it all pressing in around him. Then, with a determined breath, he stepped out, his mind already half-closed to the world and half-open to the dream that waited.

Echoes of Parting

That night, Ashlee's movements were brisk and determined as he slipped away to bed, eager for the dreams that awaited him. Julia's expression was a blend of surprise and disappointment, her eyebrows raised in silent question as she watched him retreat with the urgency of someone late for an appointment. "You're going to bed already?" Her tone was firm yet gentle, the words catching him just before he slipped out of sight. She folded her arms and sighed, the weight of her gaze following him as the door clicked shut.

The apartment was softly lit, a warm glow from the lamps giving the cluttered space a cozy feel. Julia stood in the middle of it, her presence grounded and real. "It's only nine," she continued, more to the empty room than to Ashlee. The echo of her voice carried a note of incredulity, the surprise of someone who'd thought there would be more to the evening than this.

Ashlee reappeared in the doorway, his posture half-committed to staying and half-leaning toward the bedroom. "I'm just really tired," he offered, a touch of apology in his voice. His eyes met hers briefly before darting away, a silent admission that this was not the first time they'd had this exchange.

"Are you?" Her question was soft but insistent, her gaze holding his for a moment longer than he was comfortable with. She moved to the couch, picking up one of his gaming magazines and flipping through it with a distracted air. "Or are you just trying to grind experience in your dreams?" Her tone was teasing, but there was an edge to it, a sharpness that cut through the cozy ambience.

Ashlee chuckled, a sound that lacked conviction. "Maybe both?" He ran a hand through his hair, making it messier rather than neat. "I had this insane dream last night. All these game worlds mashed together. It was..." He searched for the right word, settling on the one that best captured his enthusiasm. "Epic."

Julia set the magazine down and leaned back, her expression softening but still holding a trace of the earlier disappointment. "We haven't had a night to ourselves in ages," she said, a gentle reminder of the real-world connection she craved. Her eyes held a warmth that pulled at him, even as his mind pulled him elsewhere.

He hesitated, torn between the vivid escapes he longed for and the tangible presence of his wife. "I know," he said finally, his voice quieter now, as if the admission itself were something fragile. He moved toward her, sitting on the edge of the couch with a reluctance that didn't go unnoticed. "But I'm just so wiped out today. I don't think I'd be very good company."

Julia reached for his hand, a small gesture that carried more weight than he realized. "Even your ghost is better than nothing," she said, half-smiling at her own joke. The smile faded slightly as she added, "I just miss you, Ash."

Her words hung between them, a gentle accusation wrapped in care. Ashlee squeezed her hand, the warmth of it pulling him back to the present. "I miss you too," he said, and he meant it, but the distance he felt was more than physical. He wanted to explain it, to put into words how the dreams had become something more than an escape, but the effort seemed too great, the language of it too foreign.

"I know this is your thing," Julia said, giving his hand a reassuring squeeze before letting go. "Your passion." She leaned forward, her expression a blend of understanding and need. "But I want us to be a team, not just two players in different games."

Ashlee nodded, his eyes tracing the patterns on the rug as if they might lead him to the right response. "We are," he said, almost a question. His own uncertainty startled him. "It's just...I can't explain it. The dreams, they feel..." He paused, looking for the right analogy. "Like an alternate reality. Something I have to explore."

"Then take me with you," Julia said, her voice both tender and firm. "I want to be part of your quests, even if it's just cheering you on from the sidelines."

Her words stirred something in him, an acknowledgment of the depth of her patience and the reality of her presence. He stood, the movement abrupt but not unkind, and kissed her on the forehead. "I promise we'll have a real night soon. You can tank, and I'll be the healer." The gaming metaphor was meant to bridge the gap, to remind them both of the roles they played, but it fell short, leaving an echo of its failure in the air.

Julia watched him as he backed away, her eyes a mixture of acceptance and resignation. "I'm holding you to that," she said, her voice carrying the weight of her hope and the lightness of her resignation. She picked up the magazine again, flipping to a random page without really seeing it. Her presence filled the room even as his absence began to creep in, the quiet of the apartment settling like dust on an unused console.

Ashlee hovered in the doorway, his silhouette outlined by the soft glow of the bedroom light. "Goodnight, Julia," he said, the words both a farewell and an apology. He watched her for a moment longer, as if imprinting the scene in his mind. Then, with a final glance at the woman who remained, he turned away, letting the door click softly shut behind him.

The dreams waited, a vivid chaos he longed to return to, but the reality he'd left behind was its own complex world, one he'd yet to fully understand. Julia's sigh reached him even through the closed door, and it carried the weight of a pause button, a life on hold until he could figure out how to hit continue.

VII
Mastering the Games

Between Pixels and Heartbeats

The glow of five screens washed over Ashlee like moonlight, lending his cluttered apartment a surreal air. He sat at the epicenter, hunched but focused, as if the seat of some futuristic chariot, guiding digital steeds across virtual plains. Posters of mythical landscapes gazed down like curious gods while the rapid clack of keys and staccato controller clicks filled the room with a mechanical symphony. Ashlee's fingers moved with improbable precision, and his eyes were wide with the thrill of battle as Marcus exclaimed over the headset, "Great move, Ashlee!" Snacks and energy drinks littered the room, evidence of a marathon session, but he seemed untouched by fatigue, absorbed in the electrifying now of the game.

A hollow metallic clang rang out, and Ashlee winced, his avatar barely dodging a lethal strike. "Watch it, watch it!" Marcus's voice crackled through the headphones, urgency mixing with amusement. The clamor of the digital battlefield surrounded Ashlee, and his fingers danced across the keyboard with an elegance that defied his hunched posture. "I've got it," Ashlee replied, his words confident but soft, mirroring his calm amidst the chaos. He weaved his character through a labyrinth of enemy fire, coordinating with Marcus in a silent language of button taps and screen blinks.

"He's going for it," Marcus announced, anticipation bubbling in his tone. Ashlee grinned, feeling the growing energy as he executed a precisely timed parry, turning an enemy's attack against them in a flash of in-game brilliance. "Got him," he breathed, his eyes fixed on the screen, reflecting the vivid colors of their digital triumph. Marcus laughed, a sound of pure enjoyment. "Great move, Ashlee! Seriously, where did that come from?"

Ashlee allowed himself a small smile, feeling a surge of pride and confidence that was almost tangible. The focus and intensity of the game created a bubble around him, and for once, he felt entirely in control.

His apartment stood in stark contrast to the crisp lines of the virtual world. Posters of fantastical realms hung slightly askew on the walls, peering down at Ashlee's cluttered sanctuary. Energy drink cans formed a haphazard army along the desk, flanking a half-eaten pizza and an array of snack wrappers that bore witness to long hours of gaming. The room was a monument to Ashlee's passions and his tendency to lose himself in them completely, yet it had a warmth that was entirely his own.

The tournament raged on, and Ashlee's mastery was a beacon, guiding his team through the storm. "He's mine," Ashlee declared, his voice steady as he dispatched another opponent with a series of well-aimed hits. "Ashlee is unstoppable today," Marcus marveled, awe creeping into his words as Ashlee's precise maneuvers opened pathways for their teammates.

Ashlee felt the words wrapping around him, his self-doubt beginning to crumble under their weight. He was here, fully present, and thriving in this world where his talents translated directly into victory. Every keystroke was a brushstroke in a masterpiece of tactics, and Ashlee reveled in the clarity and purpose of it all.

"Watch out, two more at your nine o'clock," Marcus warned, but there was a note of playful respect now, as if Ashlee had become something more than a teammate. Ashlee acknowledged with a quick nod, his attention a laser beam as he led their team in another aggressive push. The keyboard clattered beneath his fingers, a rapid tattoo that harmonized with the game's relentless rhythm.

"Marcus, circle around; I've got them distracted," Ashlee instructed, his commands precise and self-assured. Marcus responded instantly, their coordination reaching new heights as Ashlee's tactics set the stage for a flawless victory.

"Whoa, nice strat!" Marcus shouted, admiration unmasked as they finished the round. Ashlee felt the glow of it, brighter than the screens, lifting him higher. "Did you install some hacks or something?" Marcus joked, but the admiration in his voice was genuine. Ashlee chuckled, a rare sound that mingled with the virtual fanfare of another triumph.

"Just the usual patches," Ashlee replied, his words laced with a dry humor that was seldom heard outside these moments. His eyes sparkled with the victory, his connection with Marcus a lifeline to something real and affirming.

They dove into the next match, and Ashlee's world was a fusion of sights and sounds, all colored by the thrilling edge of competition. His apartment was a kingdom of untamed clutter, his mind a realm of ordered strategy, and in these spaces, Ashlee felt an uncommon freedom. "Here we go again," he murmured, his voice lost beneath the game's roar but resonant with determination.

He could almost see Marcus's grin in Singapore, a continent away, as they continued to dominate the field. "Ashlee, you should do this more often," Marcus suggested between plays, his voice as vibrant as ever. "The team is loving it."

"I might just have to," Ashlee replied, the thought of being more than just a shadow in this community filling him with an unexpected warmth.

The matches blurred together, a montage of cunning plays and excited shouts. Marcus was a constant presence, his energy infectious, his respect for Ashlee's new prowess evident in every word. "Ashlee's carrying us all today!" he exclaimed, their victories stacking up like the empty cans that lined Ashlee's room.

The thrill of it wrapped around Ashlee like a living thing, more real than the clutter of his desk, more potent than the sleep he'd been losing. He lingered in the afterglow of their final match, the headset slipping to his shoulders as he basked in the day's triumphs.

The muted hum of his apartment settled back into focus, but Ashlee's mind was still racing with the echoes of the games. He had been a hero today, a leader in a world he loved. "Let's do it again soon," Marcus typed in the chat, signing off with a cheerful "gg."

"Definitely," Ashlee replied, fingers brushing the keys with a lingering satisfaction. The room was still, but his thoughts were vibrant and alive. He felt a rush of anticipation for the next time, the next victory, and for the first time, the real world seemed like a place he could carry this success into.

The screens dimmed to their idle glow, casting soft shadows that mingled with the colorful clutter. Ashlee looked around, seeing the familiar mess with new eyes, and allowed himself a small, knowing smile.

Cracks in the Facade

The community center was an island of fluorescence in the midst of a grey city block, pulsing with the bright energy of competition and camaraderie. Ashlee stepped inside, blinking against the wash of light and sound, the air humming with a joyous sense of battle. Tim's handiwork was evident in every corner, from the neatly arranged rows of monitors to the eager participants clutching controllers like digital gladiators. Ashlee's entrance was almost unnoticed, his presence an unassuming shadow against the lively backdrop. Yet, with a spark of newfound confidence and a playful glint in his eye, he joined the fray, taking on the lineup with a series of swift victories that left even Tim in good-natured disbelief. "You must be cheating!" Tim exclaimed, as Ashlee's unexpected mastery took center stage.

The room buzzed with the sounds of pixelated punches and virtual explosions, each match a mini-saga in the world of Super Smash Bros. Tim moved among the players, his energy a guiding force, shouting encouragements and organizing the brackets with a joyful precision. He waved at Ashlee, a wide grin breaking across his face, the scholar's glasses glinting under the fluorescent lights. Ashlee approached, the spirit of the competition wrapping around him, a colorful cloak that lifted his already buoyant mood.

The lineup was long and daunting, a parade of local challengers ready to prove their mettle. Ashlee took his place in the queue, his earlier gaming success echoing in his mind, infusing him with a cool determination. The clatter and clamor of the tournament were a stark contrast to the solitude of his apartment, but Ashlee found himself drawn to the vibrant chaos.

With deft fingers and a calm focus, Ashlee quickly dispatched his first opponent. The thrill of the in-person challenge coursed through him like electricity, every win a testament to his growing confidence. "Who's next?" he called, a touch of humor in his voice as he readied himself for the next round.

The center was a riot of action, the walls vibrating with the kinetic energy of youth and pixels. Lines of chairs hosted intense, leaning figures, faces washed in the vivid colors of screens. Tim darted between setups, offering advice and playful taunts, his presence a kinetic pulse that drove the event forward. Ashlee sat at the edge of this swirling world, watching and waiting, absorbing the buzz with a calm that belied his usual self.

More matches came, and Ashlee's fingers found the rhythm of the game. He moved through the brackets with a smooth grace that surprised even himself, each victory adding to the chorus of cheers that filled the room. The screen flashed with his name again and again, a banner of his newfound skill and confidence.

Tim clapped him on the back as Ashlee readied for another match, his eyes bright with admiration and surprise. "Look at you go, man! You've been practicing, huh?" Ashlee just smiled, the praise mingling with the sounds of the tournament, a symphony that made him feel alive and present.

They sat side by side at the next console, their avatars leaping and dodging on the screen with frantic energy. Tim leaned in, competitive fire mixing with genuine camaraderie. "Ready to lose?" he teased, fingers already a blur on the controls. Ashlee responded with a smirk, meeting Tim's quick maneuvers with even quicker counters.

Their match was a highlight, drawing onlookers who clustered around to watch. "You must be cheating!" Tim laughed as Ashlee's relentless attacks left him struggling to keep up. Ashlee said nothing, his focus intense, but his eyes danced with a joy that needed no words.

In the din of their showdown, Ashley T's voice rang out, carrying her trademark enthusiasm. "Go, Ashlee! Show him how it's done!" she cheered, her face a beacon of excitement in the crowd. She leaned in close to the action, every win eliciting a cheer, every near miss a gasp.

Ashlee absorbed the energy, the shouts and laughter weaving into a tapestry of support and community. It was a world away from his quiet gaming nights, a world where he was becoming someone more than just a lone player in the dark.

The final moments of the match played out in a blur, Ashlee's avatar delivering a knockout blow that sent Tim's character flying off the screen. The room erupted in cheers, the sound enveloping Ashlee like a warm embrace. Tim shook his head, feigning disbelief but smiling wide. "Seriously, man, you are on fire! How'd you get so good?"

"I guess I just leveled up," Ashlee replied, his voice light with humor and satisfaction. He felt the weight of the controller in his hands, real and solid, a symbol of his unexpected success and the connections it forged.

The tournament continued, but the frenzy began to mellow as players wrapped up their games, trading stories of epic wins and close losses. Ashley T bounded over, her energy as contagious as ever. "I didn't know you had it in you!" she exclaimed, her eyes sparkling with delight. "You're like a gaming ninja!"

Ashlee shrugged, but the pride was evident in his smile. He had conquered the competition, yes, but more importantly, he had felt the embrace of this community, the warmth of shared passions and friendships. "Thanks," he said, meeting her gaze with a newfound openness. "It was fun."

As the event wound down, Ashlee lingered in the afterglow of the day's triumphs. Tim and Ashley T's voices mingled with the fading sounds of the games, a soft echo of camaraderie and support. The bright energy of the room lingered with him as he stepped back out into the grey of the city, a glowing reminder that the real world had its own kind of victories.

Dissonance in the Daylight

The soft whir of a dozen computers whispered through the modest office, a sound that usually settled around Ashlee like a comfortable old sweater. Today, it was a distant murmur, overshadowed by the vibrant echoes of recent victories. Student files crowded his desk, looming over him like neglected sentinels, but his thoughts were a world away, still tangled in combos and conquests. Chen Laoshi appeared at the door, her presence a sharp contrast to his distracted haze. "Ashlee, may I have a word?" Her voice was gentle but insistent, cutting through the digital fog. She regarded him with a careful eye, noticing the shadows beneath his lids and the slight tremor in his hand. "Are you alright at home?" she inquired, her concern genuine. Ashlee deflected with a quick "I'm fine," his gaze skimming the papers without really seeing them, the glow of recent successes blinding him to the world at hand.

The office was a landscape of subdued colors and soft rustles, a world away from the explosive hues and sounds of the gaming tournaments. Papers shifted quietly on the desks, whispers of responsibility that called to Ashlee but found no response. The ceiling lights cast a gentle glow, more restraint than the electric pulse of the screens he was used to. The entire space breathed with a quiet life, but Ashlee remained apart from it, a distracted observer caught in a daydream.

Chen Laoshi stepped inside, her business attire a crisp contrast to the cluttered mess of Ashlee's desk. Her expression was a blend of professionalism and genuine concern, eyes sharp as they took in his disheveled state. She paused, letting the silence settle before speaking again. "Ashlee, you seem... distant," she said, choosing her words with her usual care. Her reading glasses perched on top of her head, forgotten in the face of more pressing matters.

"I'm here," Ashlee replied, a touch defensively, though his attention was clearly not. The truth was, his mind still roamed the battlefields of Elden Ring and the vibrant chaos of the community center. The clarity and excitement of those moments left everything else feeling muted, flat.

Chen tilted her head slightly, her dry humor surfacing in her next words. "Physically, perhaps," she said, her tone softening as she folded her arms, her demeanor that of a mentor concerned for her charge. "But you seem preoccupied. Is there something on your mind?"

Ashlee hesitated, caught between the allure of his digital triumphs and the nagging pull of the real world. He shuffled some papers, the action more a diversion than a task. "I'm fine, really," he repeated, his voice lacking the conviction to make it true.

The office spoke in gentle murmurs, the distant hum of other staff providing a backdrop to the uneasy silence that stretched between them. Ashlee's desk was a landscape of forgotten duties, each paper a reminder of the balance he was failing to maintain. Yet he couldn't summon the focus, the will to engage with it.

Chen's concern didn't waver, though her questions shifted. "Perhaps you're just in need of rest?" she suggested, noting the weary lines that traced Ashlee's face. "You've been putting in long hours."

He almost laughed at that, the irony of where his time was truly spent a secret he kept poorly. "It's nothing," Ashlee said, brushing away her worry with a wave of his hand, a gesture that mirrored his disregard for the work piling up around him.

Chen studied him, her silence filled with understanding and something like pity. "You're a valuable part of this team," she began, her voice deliberate and careful. "I hope you know that."

Ashlee nodded, but the words slipped off him, unable to find purchase in his distracted state. His thoughts were still consumed by the screen-lit victories, by the newfound sense of achievement that those virtual worlds had given him.

"Maybe we might consider a different approach," Chen continued, her gentle way of pointing out his faltering performance. "If you ever need help, you know where to find me."

Her kindness was almost a rebuke, but Ashlee felt only a vague discomfort, a sense that the real world was encroaching on his carefully maintained illusions. He muttered a half-hearted agreement, already turning back to the unyielding stack of files, his eyes drifting out of focus.

The office remained patient, waiting for him to return to its fold. The steady hum of the computer was a lullaby, tempting him to slip back into old routines, but Ashlee was restless, pulled between the exhilarating victories of his gaming and the heavy expectations that sat like leaden weights on his desk.

Chen watched him for a moment longer, as if weighing her words, then turned to leave. Her footsteps were a soft echo, a reminder of the reality he was failing to engage with, of the world that needed more than he seemed willing to give.

The door clicked shut behind her, and Ashlee was alone again, but the sense of victory that had buoyed him was beginning to wane. He picked up a file, stared at it without seeing, then let it fall back to the desk. His thoughts refused to settle, a constant swirl of tactical maneuvers and bright screen flashes.

He leaned back in his chair, exhaustion creeping in at the edges of his determined focus. The adrenaline of the tournaments was a fading echo, leaving a silence that felt almost accusatory. He knew Chen was right, that he was letting things slip, but the thrill of his newfound success was addictive, a siren call that was hard to ignore.

The office continued its quiet vigil, waiting, always waiting, as Ashlee's divided attention drifted further away.

VIII

The Ultimatum

A Glimpse of Truth

Julia stood in the doorway with her arms crossed and her eyes narrowed. Ashlee glanced up from the glow of his computer screen, barely aware she had come in. He didn't even have a chance to fumble an apology. "Either you cut back on your gaming and get help, or I'm leaving," she declared, her voice echoing with both hurt and determination.

Ashlee turned in his chair, stunned, his fingers pausing mid-keystroke. She had traded the elegance of a dinner party for the starkness of an ultimatum, and it hit him like a punch. He opened his mouth, then closed it, struggling to find words. "Julia, I—"

"Do you even remember what you missed?" Julia's voice was firm, her expression a portrait of disbelief. Her dress, professional and polished, was meant for an evening out, not a showdown in their living room.

He blinked rapidly, trying to adjust to this unexpected confrontation. "The dinner," he said, almost to himself. "I thought it was next week."

She exhaled sharply, a mix of frustration and exasperation. "Next week? Do you even realize how much I needed you there tonight? Wei Lin was asking about you."

"Lin? I—" Ashlee felt like his mind was buffering. He had forgotten more than just the dinner; he had forgotten everything tied to it. "I just got caught up in—"

"Gaming. Again." Julia's interruption was as sharp as her gaze. "You're always caught up in gaming, Ashlee."

He looked down, guilty and defensive, searching for something that wouldn't sound like the same old excuse. "This update is huge, Julia. I'm talking groundbreaking. I lost track of time."

"You always lose track of time." She was hurt, the kind of hurt that had been building over missed dates and lonely nights. "You can't even remember what day it is anymore. Do you think that's okay?"

Ashlee rubbed the back of his neck, his posture slumping further under her scrutiny. "I didn't think it was that serious. I mean, you know how these things get with deadlines and patches."

Julia unfolded her arms, stepping into the room with a purposeful stride. "And what about our deadlines, Ashlee? Our patches?" Her tone was tinged with sarcasm, yet there was a tremor beneath it that revealed how close to breaking she felt.

He stood up, more rattled than he wanted to admit. "I'm sorry, Julia. Really. It's just—this world makes sense to me. It's... predictable."

"And I don't?" Her words hung in the air, more question than accusation.

"No, that's not what I meant." Ashlee took a step toward her, his voice growing more urgent. "I love you. You know that. I just—sometimes it's like I need to escape. It's not about you. It's me."

"That's the problem, Ashlee." Her eyes softened, just a bit, but her resolve didn't waver. "It's always about you."

He could feel her slipping away, not physically, but emotionally. It scared him. He reached for her hand, his touch a silent plea for her to understand. It was trembling, a mirror of his own fear and longing.

For a moment, the world held its breath.

Then, without warning, a shimmering cascade of light enveloped them. It poured over them like a wave, rippling with warmth and color. The familiar clutter of their apartment dissolved, pixel by pixel, into something entirely new.

Suddenly, they were outside, the air filled with the soft sounds of a virtual paradise. A gentle digital breeze rustled through the pastel hues of a quaint village. Wooden benches and flowering trees dotted the landscape. It was serene, inviting, nothing like the tense scene moments before.

Ashlee and Julia stood in the heart of this unexpected realm, the shock still plain on their faces. The ambient hum of a virtual stream whispered in the background, as if mocking the silence between them.

Julia looked around, her earlier fury muted by the cozy environment. "What just happened?" she asked, a mix of disbelief and awe.

Ashlee glanced at their intertwined hands, then back at her. The conflict was still there, lingering, but now something else was emerging: curiosity. "I think," he said, hesitating to believe it himself, "we're in the game."

They were suspended in this new space, surrounded by a world that felt soft and welcoming, as unreal as a dream but as vivid as a memory. The pastel trees swayed gently, and the benches looked inviting under the pink-tinted sky. Julia's gaze shifted from angry to thoughtful, her mind as engaged as her senses. Ashlee, too, seemed caught between emotions, the urgency of their earlier confrontation giving way to a tentative sense of wonder.

As they stood there, their expressions were a mix of everything unresolved and everything possible, hanging in the balance of this enchanting pause.

Threads of Memory

Sunlight filtered through the pixelated leaves, casting playful shadows on the cobblestone paths. Ashlee and Julia stood in a bright clearing, their hands still clasped, as if holding on for dear life. The quaintness of the Animal Crossing village surrounded them with a quiet charm. Slowly, they began to talk.

Julia looked at Ashlee, the earlier fury fading into something more contemplative. "Are we really in the game?" she asked, her voice holding a mixture of wonder and disbelief.

Ashlee nodded, glancing around. "I think we are." He was as surprised as she was, but a small part of him felt a thrill. He gave her hand a gentle squeeze, testing the reality of their shared moment.

They stood in silence for a moment, the kind that was both awkward and peaceful. Around them, pastel houses with flower boxes sat comfortably next to each other, each with its own rustic charm. The trees swayed slightly in the virtual breeze, and a tiny stream meandered nearby, adding a soft background hum.

Ashlee finally spoke, breaking the quiet spell. "How are you feeling about all this?" His tone was tentative, as if unsure whether to celebrate or apologize.

Julia hesitated, glancing at the surroundings. The soft hues and welcoming design seemed to work their magic on her tension. "It's... a lot to take in," she admitted, her lips curving into an involuntary half-smile. "But it's strangely calming."

They began to walk, letting the cozy atmosphere lead them down a cobblestone path. Wooden signs with cheerful messages dotted the way, and an occasional digital villager waved as they passed. It was the kind of place that felt as inviting as an old friend's living room.

"You spend all your time here, don't you?" Julia asked, the question more understanding than accusatory.

Ashlee nodded, a little sheepishly. "It's easy to get lost. I never thought you'd see it like this."

Her earlier anger softened further, replaced by curiosity. "I finally understand what you've been going through," she said, glancing at him with sincerity. "I never knew it felt like this."

He looked at her, relief and hope mingling in his eyes. "It's not just about escape, Julia. It's about creating something. Being a part of it. It's... freeing."

They stopped by a flowering tree, the digital petals falling like promises. Ashlee hesitated before continuing. "I know I've been gone too much, even when I'm here. I didn't realize how much it was hurting you."

Julia touched the tree trunk, her fingers brushing against the textures that felt both real and surreal. "It's not just me," she said softly. "It's us. I miss us."

Ashlee felt a pang of guilt, sharper than any he'd felt in a while. "I'm sorry," he said, his voice barely a whisper. "I didn't know how to balance it all. But I want to try."

They walked on, the gentle murmur of digital life enveloping them like a favorite blanket. A tiny pond reflected the pastel sky, and a wooden bench invited them to sit, though they chose to keep moving.

Julia's expression was thoughtful, her practical nature blending with a newfound openness. "I know you need this," she said, nodding at the world around them. "But we need you, too."

He gave her a tentative smile, hope rekindling in his heart. "I can find a way to be in both worlds. I will. I promise."

The path led them past cozy cottages, each with a charm that whispered of possibility. The conversation grew more intimate, their words like stepping stones toward reconnection.

"You know, there are ways to escape that don't mean shutting everything else out," Julia said, her tone gently teasing. "Maybe we can set some boundaries."

Ashlee's eyes lit up with a mix of relief and joy. "I'd like that," he said, the smile on his face growing. "A lot."

The occasional squeeze of her hand and the warmth in her eyes told him he was understood, maybe for the first time in a long while. "I just need to know we're doing this together," she said.

"We are," Ashlee promised. "Completely."

The coziness of the game world seemed to hold them in a safe, timeless space, where possibilities felt endless. Even the virtual villagers seemed to sense the shift, their routines carrying on in the background like a serene soundtrack to their moment.

"I think we can make this work," Julia said, her confidence returning. "But couples counseling wouldn't hurt."

Ashlee chuckled, a sound of agreement and affection. "If it means keeping you, I'm all in."

The digital magic gradually faded, the colors of the quaint village dissolving into the familiar tones of their apartment. They were back, but with something new—a shared understanding and a renewed promise.

Julia looked at him, her gaze softer now. "So," she said, "boundaries?"

He nodded eagerly. "And help. I'll get it. Really."

Their commitment felt as solid as the handhold that connected them. It was a beginning, one that felt as cozy and full of promise as the world they had just left behind.

IX

The Hidden Truth

Into the Unknown

The heat of the explosion rippled against Ashlee's avatar, nearly forcing him to drop his controller as he parried the giant's blow. He leaned forward, hyper-focused, every muscle in his body tight as the screen in front of him erupted with dazzling chaos. "Nice move, Ashlee!" shouted Marcus as the din of swords clashing filled his dimly lit apartment. Even from miles away, his friend's voice crackled with intensity through his headset. Ashlee's heart raced, his sense of the physical world dissolving with every precise move. He was there—in the gritty trenches of Elden Ring—surrounded by howling beasts, forgotten castles, and towering, fire-breathing enemies that blurred so vividly against the dark he could almost smell the smoke.

Ashlee's thumbs flew over the controller, a seamless dance of buttons and triggers that propelled his knight through the fray. "Keep it up, guys! He's almost down!" Marcus urged, his tone brimming with adrenaline. Ashlee shot back, his voice animated, "Watch my six; there's another coming!" Their coordination was a symphony of precision, each member of the clan syncing perfectly in the digital melee. Ashlee felt the controller vibrate with each sword clash and arrow thud, the rhythmic feedback intensifying his connection to the battle. The glow from the screen bathed his face, but all he saw was the epic struggle unfolding within.

Metallic clinks filled his ears as Ashlee's avatar engaged the enemy, his breathing syncing with the game's escalating tempo. A guttural roar echoed through the headset as a beast lunged forward, and Ashlee's fingers moved instinctively, sidestepping the attack with milliseconds to spare. He felt every movement as if it were his own—every heavy footfall and graceful parry, every bead of sweat and jolt of adrenaline. The virtual armor on his knight seemed to weigh on him, pressing against his shoulders as the world around him blurred into visceral immersion.

Graphics flashed across the screen, vivid and lifelike: mighty dragons wheeling through stormy skies, crumbling castles shrouded in mist, and swirling snow mingling with the blaze of battle. Ashlee was so deeply absorbed that he could feel the heat of the fire, the chill of the night, the wind rattling his visor. Marcus's voice cut through the tumult again, a beacon of excitement. "Ashlee, the big guy's all yours! Make it count!" With a grin tugging at his lips, Ashlee sent his knight charging into the fray, his concentration fierce, unwavering. He was the hero, the legend, the knight on the frontlines of war.

Years of gaming had led him to this moment, honed his skills to a razor's edge. Once a casual player, now a dedicated warrior in this digital realm, Ashlee maneuvered his avatar with dexterous expertise. His fingers were a blur, executing commands with split-second timing as he deftly sidestepped and countered, engaging in a dance of destruction with the onslaught of enemies. Marcus's voice broke in with shouted strategies, echoing a trust built over countless missions together. "Don't let up, push forward!" Ashlee absorbed every word, his senses tingling with the rush of battle.

His bond with Marcus and the clan played out in vibrant bursts of action and rapid-fire dialogue, a tapestry of camaraderie that felt as real as any face-to-face interaction. They communicated in a language of gamers, a dialect of callouts and jests that transcended the miles. "Where'd you learn that move?" Marcus teased, to which Ashlee retorted with playful swagger, "Pro strats, my friend." Connected through cables and codes, he felt the pulse of their shared adventure, the thrill of belonging to something bigger than himself.

The screen filled with dazzling chaos as the fight reached a crescendo, each swing of his digital sword a masterstroke, each dodge a dance of survival. Ashlee's grip tightened on the controller, every nerve alive with sensation. The sheer intensity of the gaming flooded his mind, washing away the dim apartment, the sounds of the city, and the clutter of everyday life. He was lost to the world—immersed, engulfed—every thought and breath consumed by the epic clash before him.

His perception of the virtual and the real continued to meld, dissolving the boundary between pixels and physicality. The more he played, the more tangible it all felt: the ground vibrating beneath his feet, the sting of cold wind, the rhythm of his heart pounding in unison with the game's tempo. He was there, truly there, his senses enveloped by the gritty, raw intensity of the Elden Ring universe.

"That was legendary!" Marcus's voice rang out, congratulatory and breathless, as the final foe fell. Ashlee exhaled, the room around him slowly reasserting itself against the retreating echoes of the battle. He sank back into his chair, fingers tingling from the frenzy. "We crushed it," he agreed, feeling the lingering warmth of the game world as he tore his eyes from the screen. It had been a triumphant run, and the virtual lands felt more like home with every session. He sat there a moment longer, letting the victory sink in, reluctant to step back into the stillness of the room.

The Edge of Perception

The dust was still settling on the battlefield when Ashlee's avatar slipped away, each footstep echoing in the hush of the abandoned game clearing. Wind sighed softly through the crumbling stone ruins, carrying a faint, digital chill. The vibrant colors of the moss seemed to glow with an otherworldly brightness against the ruins' grey, and his heart drummed with adrenaline as the eerie calm enveloped him. He was alone, he thought. And then the voice came. Measured. Intentional. It broke the silence with a name: "Ashlee."

Eldred's tone was calm and composed, cutting through the residual roar of battle. Ashlee paused, surprise rippling through him. Who was this character? How did it know his name? His avatar turned, scanning the ruined clearing with cautious curiosity. At first, the sage seemed part of the landscape, a hooded figure among the stone and moss. But then he moved, a slight incline of the head, and Ashlee's breath caught. Eldred's presence was both simple and imposing, a stark contrast to the chaos left behind in the virtual trenches. Ashlee was riveted, drawn in by the enigmatic figure's deliberate appearance.

"What is this?" Ashlee's voice crackled with a mix of suspicion and wonder, as though he himself stood within the clearing. The words came again, calm and unwavering, echoing with a strange authority that tugged at his thoughts. "Your gift is not singular, Ashlee; others traverse these worlds, and some walk darker paths." Eldred's eyes seemed to pierce through the digital veil, holding Ashlee's gaze with unnerving intensity. The unexpected encounter sent a jolt of intrigue through him, stirring a swirl of excitement and doubt.

Ashlee found himself responding to Eldred, the questions tumbling out as if spoken to an old mentor. "What do you mean? What paths? How do you know this?" His own voice surprised him, full of urgency and hunger for answers. Eldred's words came measured, each one a piece of a puzzle that danced tantalizingly beyond Ashlee's reach. "There are those who would use your ability for their own ends," the sage continued, his speech deliberate against the soft clink of weaponry and the ghostly whisper of wind. "And those who would seek to stop them." Tension wove through the silence, electrifying the air with possibility.

The revelation sank in, weaving its way through Ashlee's mind like an intricate game plot unfolding in real time. Could there really be others like him? Was there truly a sinister group crossing both digital and real worlds? The answers seemed just out of reach, teasing him with both promise and danger. As Ashlee absorbed Eldred's words, he felt excitement and uncertainty knotting within him, leaving him dazed yet eager to discover more. The sage's voice lingered, wrapping around him like a haunting refrain, until the clearing began to shudder with foreboding intensity.

The scene shifted, the digital clarity blurring around Ashlee's senses. He felt his vision dim, the ruins and moss dissolving into pixelated fog. A final flicker of Eldred's form—shadowy, resolute—and Ashlee snapped back to his dimly lit apartment. He blinked against the harsh return to reality, the game's ghostly echoes still vibrating in his mind. The familiar clutter of his desk and the distant hum of city life surrounded him, but everything felt thin, insubstantial, a pale shadow of the world he had just left. The transition was jarring, and he sat there, blinking into the murky room.

His phone buzzed insistently, pulling his attention away from the lingering visions of Eldred. A glance at the screen showed missed calls—dozens of them—all from Julia. Ashlee's heart lurched as he opened the notifications, her worried messages unfolding like an urgent timeline of concern. She was trying to reach him, and from the looks of it, had been for some time. Just as he was about to call her back, the phone vibrated in his hand, Julia's image filling the display with a concerned expression. He hesitated a moment, feeling the surreal dissonance between game and reality, then answered.

"Ashlee! Finally. I've been trying to reach you for over an hour." Her voice carried a mix of relief and frustration, grounded and clear against his still-whirling thoughts. He struggled to form words, the afterimage of Eldred's revelation overlapping with the reality of Julia's worry. "Sorry, I was—caught up," he replied, the understatement nearly making him laugh at its inadequacy. "Are you okay? It felt like you'd disappeared off the face of the Earth," Julia continued, her tone softening. Ashlee's mind raced to bridge the gap between the game world and her pressing concern.

"I'm... fine. Just lost track of time," he offered, his voice distant as he glanced at the paused game screen, its frozen image a stark reminder of what he'd just experienced. Julia sighed, the sound patient yet exasperated. "Well, I'm on my way. We'll talk then," she said, the determination in her voice a comfort. Ashlee nodded, the gesture more to himself than to her. "I'll be here," he replied, wondering if that was really true in the sense she meant.

The call ended, and Ashlee sat in the quiet, letting the silence stretch around him. Julia's impending visit loomed in his thoughts, but so did the shadowy hints of Eldred's message. Wonder and concern tangled together, leaving him perched on the edge of something he couldn't quite name. He glanced again at the paused screen, the digital world waiting like a half-remembered dream, then turned his eyes toward the window, watching the city blink against the night as he waited for Julia to arrive.

X

Doubt and Dilemma

Forging Bonds

Ashlee's fingers danced lethargically across the keyboard, barely tapping in time with the half-hearted rhythm of his mind. The glow of the monitor cast him in shades of pale blues and greens, making his usual unkempt appearance seem even more rumpled. A noisy fan whirred from the corner of the room, struggling against the growing heat of his gaming setup as if it, too, were losing the will to fight. Tim appeared in the doorway like a gust of fresh air, armed with a broad smile and a bag full of energy drinks. "Come on, buddy, let's kick it into high gear!" he shouted, his enthusiasm clashing with Ashlee's sluggish moves. Ashlee's response was as distracted as his gameplay, his character staggering on screen while his focus seemed tied down by invisible weights.

Tim crossed the room with bouncing steps, set down his gear on the cluttered coffee table, and peered at Ashlee's screen. "Is that you playing, or did you let a three-year-old take over?" he teased, tapping Ashlee's shoulder. Ashlee shrugged, mumbling, "Yeah, yeah, I'm a little rusty." The room felt warm and cluttered, game cases and empty soda cans scattered like the remnants of Ashlee's recent gaming marathons. Tim plopped onto the couch, his energy filling the space. "Rusty's an understatement. Where's your A-game, man? We need to marathon this weekend. I even brought reinforcements." He waved an energy drink enticingly.

Ashlee attempted a half-smile, his attention still mostly on the screen. "Maybe later. I'm kind of busy." Tim leaned back, clearly puzzled. "Busy doing what? Missing all your targets?" His laughter was friendly but insistent, trying to shake Ashlee out of his stupor. Ashlee's character faltered again, and he sighed, letting his hands drop from the keyboard. The defeat in his virtual battle mirrored the growing tension between the two friends. The silence of Ashlee's pause spoke louder than his words, hinting at something deeper.

Julia's entrance was soft but sure, her heels clicking gently on the hardwood floor as she came up behind them. "Ashlee," she said, her voice carrying both warmth and a hint of reproach. "We need to talk." Her eyes flickered from Ashlee to the screen, noticing his poorly executed moves with a knowing look. Ashlee glanced back, looking caught, and then at Tim, whose enthusiasm wavered in the charged atmosphere. "Julia," Ashlee started, but she interrupted, her tone firm but caring. "You can't keep ignoring real life. This is serious." Her presence added a new weight to the room, the conversation shifting as Tim picked up on the tension.

Tim scratched his head, clearly uncomfortable with the new direction. "Uh, maybe I should come back later?" he offered, trying to read the room. Ashlee looked torn, stuck between Tim's carefree spirit and Julia's urgent concern. "No, it's fine," Ashlee said, his voice lacking conviction. "We're just—" Julia cut him off, her determination undeterred. "We can't keep putting this off, Ashlee. Things have to change." She glanced at Tim, softening slightly. "It's not just a game." Her words hit with unexpected clarity, each sentence drawing the contrast between Ashlee's world and hers.

Tim gave a sheepish grin, backing towards the door. "Guess I really should have called first, huh?" His humor was an attempt to lighten the mood, though it only partially succeeded. Ashlee looked at the floor, his hands twitching as if they couldn't decide whether to reach for the keyboard or not. "I'll be back tomorrow," Tim said, more gently this time. "We'll have that marathon, and you'll be ready, right?" He gave Ashlee a knowing nod, his optimism unfaltering even as he retreated.

Julia watched Tim leave, her eyes softening as she turned back to Ashlee. "I know how much you love this," she said, gesturing to the glowing screen, "but it's getting in the way of everything else. You need to find a balance." Her concern was genuine, filling the room like a tangible presence. Ashlee looked defeated, the slump of his shoulders more pronounced. "I'm trying," he murmured, but his words seemed to fall flat even to his own ears.

The room seemed quieter now, the absence of Tim's energy a noticeable gap. The fan's hum and the dim light cast long shadows that danced on the walls, mirroring Ashlee's internal struggle. "It doesn't feel like you are," Julia said, her voice softer now but no less insistent. Ashlee sank back into his chair, staring at the screen without really seeing it. The weight of Julia's words—and his own silence—settled over him like a thick, unyielding blanket.

He finally nodded, the movement small and uncertain. "I'll figure it out," he said, the conviction barely audible. Julia gave a reluctant but hopeful smile, squeezing his shoulder before she turned away. The door clicked softly behind her, leaving Ashlee alone in the dim room, where the digital glow cast its familiar but increasingly alien light. He sat motionless, letting the tension and worry soak into the silence.

The room, usually filled with the sounds of frantic gameplay and Ashlee's triumphant shouts, felt unnaturally quiet. The hum of the cooling fan was the only constant, struggling against both the warmth of the equipment and the heaviness of Ashlee's thoughts. His life—once synchronized perfectly with the pixelated rhythms of his games—now seemed out of sync, paused at an uncertain level with no clear strategy in sight.

XI

Virtual Infiltration

Caught in the Net

An ocean of LED light lapped at Ashlee's gaming den, cresting over his face in a wash of blues and greens. The luminescent surf parted as a message floated on screen, casting the room in ominous shadow: "Weird behavior in the clan—check it out now." His controller creaked under a tightening grip. He gulped in a lungful of air, then dived.

Instantly, he was in—the pixelated expanse of Elden Ring unfurling like a vast, familiar kingdom. The Lands Between sprawled around him, a playground of treacherous beauty. His avatar's armor clinked rhythmically as he advanced through the medieval landscape, feeling the weight of both weapon and world. It was a place that had always felt like home, more than the foreign country he lived in, more than the actual walls surrounding his computer desk. But today, something was off. Clan members dotted the landscape, their movements curiously synchronized. They forged forward with unsettling precision, attacking in eerie unison, like NPCs from an outdated quest. Ashlee watched them for a moment, puzzled, before Marcus's avatar dashed up beside him.

"Something glitched?" Ashlee typed quickly, watching KnightSlayer92's dual katanas bob in agreement.

"Crazy stuff," Marcus shot back. "Whole server seems weird. Players said you went AWOL xD." The message blinked into the chat log, underscoring Ashlee's mounting sense of dread with Marcus's trademark humor.

"Reorganizing AI?" Ashlee speculated, his fingers dancing over the keyboard. "Never seen it like this."

Marcus sent a shrug emoticon, his armored character mirroring the sentiment with a dramatic shoulder roll.

Ashlee's mind raced with possibilities, the in-game world feeling at once boundless and claustrophobic. The clan's actions were unnerving, their intentions hard to parse. He followed them, their precise movements leaving a wake of defeated enemies and abandoned loot. For the first time, the Lands Between felt foreign, almost hostile in its unfamiliarity.

Ashlee's avatar strode deeper into the game, away from the bustling hive of synchronized activity. Marcus kept pace, their virtual selves moving through the changing terrain as they tried to make sense of the bizarre situation.

"Feels like I'm in an episode of 'Players Behaving Badly,'" Marcus typed. "Spooky version. You?"

Ashlee's fingers paused, his mind snagging on the peculiarity of it all. "It's like they're... infected?" he ventured, feeling the strangeness deepen with every step.

Ahead, the landscape itself began to warp. Jagged lines blurred at the edges of Ashlee's screen, like the very fabric of the game was unraveling. The ground shifted beneath his avatar's feet, creating phantom corridors and collapsing walls. Marcus was uncharacteristically silent, his focus evident as he tackled the puzzle alongside Ashlee.

"Server hack?" Ashlee suggested, not sure whether to be impressed or alarmed.

"Maybe. Or an ARG?" Marcus replied, injecting optimism into the speculation. "Company playing mind games for new content?"

Ashlee wasn't convinced, but he admired the spin. The digital expanse felt alive, unsettlingly so. Their path through the world continued to change, the chaos making the virtual feel eerily real. The synchronized players acted with a determination that Ashlee couldn't ignore. He watched them enact the same bizarre routines in new areas, their voices detached and distant, as though reciting lines for an invisible audience.

"This is on another level," Ashlee said into the chat. "Not sure how much longer I can stick with this."

"No rage quitting, Mr. Montgomery. :P," Marcus replied, adding a winking face. "I'm AFK for food—good luck, dude." With that, Marcus's avatar bowed theatrically and vanished.

Alone now, Ashlee pressed on, his interest piqued by the unfolding mystery despite his unease. His avatar picked a path through the shifting environment, dodging traps and deciphering the growing enigma. Then, out of the glitchy haze, a corridor appeared—dark and menacing, like a crack in the world. Ashlee hesitated, the air thick with digital static.

As he neared, the passage pulsed with light and sound, an orchestra of distortion. Manipulated players filled the space, their forms flickering like corrupted data. Their armor looked splintered, as though torn from reality itself. Ashlee's hands tightened on the controller, his focus intense as he maneuvered through the chaotic scene. The ambient noise crescendoed, a chorus of glitched voices chanting in unison. It was more than he'd bargained for, each second a new revelation that spiraled further out of control.

For a brief moment, doubt crept into Ashlee's mind—was it truly just a game? Then the sensory overload struck like a tidal wave. Light, sound, and motion merged into a singular, overwhelming force. His heart pounded in his chest, each beat echoing in his ears like the world's most terrifying soundtrack. The lines between player and avatar blurred, the screen's flickering images searing into his vision. He tried to log off, his fingers frantic on the keyboard, but the digital realm had its hold on him.

Panic welled up, swallowing him as the lights swirled violently. The illusion of control shattered. Ashlee felt himself slipping, losing touch with the real world. The last thing he heard was the mechanical heartbeat of the game, beating louder, until it was the only thing left.

Then nothing.

The Reality Check

The latch clicked softly as Julia slipped into the apartment. Inside, a peculiar silence wrapped around her like an ill-fitting coat. The room flickered with the pale glow of Ashlee's computer screen, casting the absence of familiar clatter in a troubling light. Her breath snagged on uncertainty as she saw him—silent, slumped, still.

The apartment seemed to hold its breath with her as she took cautious steps forward. Ashlee's setup was a stark presence in the dim room, the high-end PC usually a symphony of keys, clicks, and muffled curses. Now it stood as a sentinel over Ashlee's unmoving form, the eerie, paused interface a chilling sentinel of its own. Julia's heart quickened, an instinctual reaction to the unsettling sight.

"Ashlee?" she ventured, voice cracking through the silence. Her eyes searched for signs of life—a flicker of his eyelids, a twitch of his fingers—but found none. His hands lay limp on the controller, his posture echoing the hours of dedication he'd poured into his gaming passion. But this wasn't the familiar scene of exhaustion. It was something else. Something worse.

"Ashlee, wake up," she urged, gently shaking his shoulder. The absence of response filled the room, more suffocating than the stillness itself. Julia swallowed, the motion too loud in the silence. Her composed exterior strained against the growing knot of fear in her chest.

A hundred thoughts collided as she stood there, paralyzed by the unfamiliar helplessness. Was he having a seizure? Had he collapsed from exhaustion? Her practical mind raced through possibilities, each one adding weight to her urgency. She looked down at him, the blue and green glow of the monitor painting his features in stark relief.

"Please, Ashlee," she said again, the plea cracking her usual composure. When the silence pushed back, she knew she couldn't wait. Her hands darted for the phone, fingers dialing with practiced precision even as her heart pounded in her ears.

"Hello, I need an ambulance," she said, voice steadying with the comfort of action. She rattled off the address, her determined professionalism underscoring the fear she refused to let in. "My husband is unresponsive," she added, each word digging a little deeper into the uncertainty she faced.

The emergency operator's voice was calm, almost surreal in its detachment. "Is he breathing?" came the first question, and Julia's eyes shot back to Ashlee's still form, searching for the rise and fall of his chest.

"Yes, but he's not waking up," she replied, hoping the words didn't betray her as much as they betrayed him.

"Can you stay with him? Help is on the way."

"Yes, I'm right here," Julia said, phone clutched tightly in her hand. Her free hand found Ashlee's shoulder again, a point of contact as much for her own reassurance as his. She stayed on the line, the operator's calm instructions guiding her through the most harrowing wait of her life. Each second was an eternity, but she remained resolute, the crisis drawing out her inner strength in ways even she hadn't anticipated.

When the call ended, Julia remained at Ashlee's side, feeling the clash of digital and real worlds echoing around her. The computer's ambient hum mixed with the blood rushing in her ears, creating a dissonant soundtrack to her mounting worry. She pulled a chair close, not willing to be more than an arm's reach away, the immediate surroundings fading into irrelevance.

"Help is coming, Ashlee," she said, the words a promise as much to herself as to him. Her gaze lingered on his face, memorizing the peacefulness she knew masked something more troubling.

As she waited, the glow from the screen seemed to pulse with an insidious life of its own. It lit the apartment in stark contrasts, each flicker emphasizing the stakes of the situation. Julia sat there, steady in her resolve, her shadow standing vigil in the wavering light. The room, the night, and her world teetered on the brink of change, but her eyes never left him, watching and willing him back to the world they shared.

XII

Stuck in the System

Old Wounds, New Battles

Monitors pulsed with persistent, anxious rhythm, casting nervous green shadows on Ashlee's pale skin. He lay on the hospital bed, silent, while the sterile room thrummed with whispered uncertainty. Julia cradled his limp hand, murmuring soft promises to his still form, her voice nearly lost beneath the antiseptic-laden air and the low hum of machines. Across the room, Tim's shoes squeaked against the polished floor as he paced, halting his frustrated march only to confer with the doctor whose brow was furrowed with confusion. Julia leaned closer, the stark lighting accentuating the concern etched into her features, her heart set on pulling Ashlee back from the threshold of this perplexing limbo.

"Ashlee, please come back," she said, her words trembling as she squeezed his hand. Her eyes never left his face, searching for any sign of movement or recognition.

Tim stopped and turned, his expression clouded with worry. He took a few hesitant steps toward Julia, pausing as if afraid to break her concentration. He watched her for a moment before addressing the doctor again, his voice filled with frustration.

"I don't understand," Tim said. "What does this mean, you've never seen anything like it?"

The doctor shifted, his own uncertainty clear. "His vitals are erratic," he repeated, as though the phrase itself might provide answers. "We're doing everything we can."

Julia brushed a lock of hair from Ashlee's forehead, her fingers gentle but urgent. The heart monitor's steady beep punctuated the silence that followed, each sound a reminder of the battle taking place within Ashlee's unresponsive form.

"I thought he was just gaming," Tim said, raking a hand through his hair. He glanced back at Julia, seeing the determination mixed with fear in her eyes. "It's never been like this before."

"Gaming?" the doctor asked, tilting his head slightly, clearly out of his depth with this particular case. He hesitated, his gaze darting between Tim and Julia. "Whatever the cause, his condition is unusual. We'll keep monitoring him closely."

Tim nodded, though the explanation offered little comfort. As the doctor left the room, his footsteps faded into the symphony of hospital sounds: the whir of machines, the distant clatter of a gurney, the whispered conversations that hovered at the edges of the sterile space.

He walked over to Julia, whose focus remained unwavering on Ashlee's face. He knelt down, placing a reassuring hand on her shoulder. "He's tough. You know him. He'll pull through."

Julia turned slightly, meeting Tim's gaze with a flicker of gratitude. Her lips formed a faint smile, though the weight of worry quickly eclipsed it. "I don't know, Tim," she said, her voice barely more than a whisper. "This isn't something he can just power through. What if...?"

"Hey, no 'what ifs,' okay?" Tim interrupted gently, giving her shoulder a soft squeeze. "You've seen him go up against some pretty tough bosses. This is no different."

His attempt at humor met with a shaky laugh, a sound that quickly dissolved back into the somber atmosphere. Julia turned her attention to Ashlee once more, the crease in her brow deepening as she wrestled with her thoughts. Her free hand trembled slightly, and Tim watched as she steadied it against the edge of the bed.

"Ashlee," she said again, her voice stronger now, laced with a mixture of love and determination. "You can't leave me here. We have so many games left to play."

Tim stood and resumed his pacing, though his movements lacked their earlier urgency. He glanced frequently at Julia, his expression softening with each pass. He wanted to say more, to find the words that would ease her mind, but all he could do was watch and wait.

"Remember when we first moved here?" Julia continued, leaning closer to Ashlee. Her voice took on a tender, nostalgic quality. "I didn't even want to buy that first console. I thought we'd be too busy to play."

Her words seemed to fill the room, resonating with a sense of shared history and connection. She smiled faintly, lost in memories of nights spent huddled around a glowing screen, of laughter and companionship that transcended the foreign world they'd chosen to inhabit.

"But you convinced me," she said, her grip tightening on his hand. "And you were right. We needed it. We needed this escape."

Tim stopped his pacing to watch her, his own memories mingling with hers. He remembered those early days, the way Ashlee's enthusiasm had bridged the gaps of culture and distance. His heart ached to see them both like this, caught in a struggle that seemed so much larger than themselves.

"We still need it," Julia said, her voice breaking slightly. "We need you, Ashlee."

Tim cleared his throat, feeling the tightness in his chest. "He can hear you," he said, his tone more subdued now. "I know he can."

Julia nodded, though the look in her eyes revealed her doubt. She released Ashlee's hand briefly to wipe a tear from her cheek, then returned it to its vigilant post, unwilling to let go for long. Her determination was palpable, a force in its own right, pushing back against the uncertainty that surrounded them.

Tim settled into a chair, his energy finally yielding to the emotional weight of the situation. He watched the monitors, the rhythmic pulsing like an unwelcome metronome ticking off the seconds. "We're not going anywhere," he said, more to himself than anyone else. "We're staying right here until you come back to us."

Julia took a deep breath, her resolve hardening with each word Tim spoke. The room's sterile confines seemed to close in around them, the antiseptic scent mingling with their collective anxiety, binding them to this moment in time.

A nurse passed by, casting a sympathetic glance their way, but no one interrupted their vigil. Even the doctor's earlier confusion was preferable to this current state of waiting, of knowing nothing and imagining everything.

The minutes dragged on, filled with quiet determination and the unending chorus of hospital sounds. Julia leaned her head against Ashlee's arm, her eyes drifting shut, exhaustion finally overcoming her. She whispered his name one last time, her breath warm against his skin, and settled into a fitful slumber.

Tim sat beside her, alert and watchful. He crossed his arms over his chest, his gaze fixed firmly on Ashlee's face. Though the mystery of Ashlee's condition hung over them like a storm cloud, Tim held on to his belief that the man he knew wouldn't give up so easily.

The hours stretched and contracted in unpredictable rhythms, bending under the weight of uncertainty. All the while, the monitors continued their relentless serenade, marking the tempo of this long, anxious wait.

Facing the Shadows

Ashlee was an electric ghost, caught between worlds that writhed and convulsed with manic purpose. He darted through a landscape where medieval armor collided with cartoon racetracks, his form flickering as if undecided which reality to haunt. A glowing sword blazed in his hands, illuminating pixelated foes and treacherous terrain. Every movement felt both exhilarating and futile, each escape route twisting into new threats. His vision glitched with dissonant clarity, the cold, clinical overlay of a heart monitor intruding on this digital mayhem. It was the ultimate raid gone wrong, and Ashlee fought against the glitching, relentless forces, even as his self began to fragment and whisper of collapse. "I can't escape," he thought, a barely audible mantra amid the chaos, his avatar slowing as hostile code closed in for the kill.

The digital landscape around him shifted like a living, breathing entity. One second, he was racing along a slick rainbow track, vibrant and chaotic; the next, he found himself amidst crumbling ruins, dark and ominous, where armored knights bore down on him with terrifying speed. His avatar, caught in the same indecisive glitch, alternated wildly between cartoonish and detailed, like two layers of reality struggling for dominance. His heart, or whatever served as its digital equivalent, pounded in his ears, synchronizing disturbingly with the distant pulse of a hospital monitor.

Ashlee leaped forward, his legs pistoning with adrenaline-fueled urgency. The bright roar of engines filled his senses as he swerved past racing karts, each vehicle a colorful threat. But even as he maneuvered with the deftness of a seasoned player, shadows loomed and the world around him fractured. In a blink, the racetrack gave way to battlegrounds littered with jagged debris and rusted metal, the hum of engines replaced by the ominous clank of armored footsteps.

His fingers gripped the hilt of the oversized sword, a weapon that crackled with electric promise. He swung it with frantic intensity, cleaving through the swarm of adversaries that coded their way toward him. Each attack sent sparks flying, a mesmerizing but ominous display that blurred the line between spectacle and threat. The entities—once pixel-perfect foes—glitched and doubled in on themselves, forming a shifting wall of opposition that left Ashlee breathless and reeling.

The landscape responded with malevolent glee, morphing and reconfiguring at a pace that left him scrambling. A fractured battleground transformed back into a treacherous raceway in the blink of an eye, and the smooth surface of the track dared him to keep pace. His avatar matched the frenetic energy, or tried to, but the reality of the situation pressed down with tangible weight. The dizzying shifts sapped his resolve, and he felt his coherence slip, his virtual form flickering with uncertainty.

Then came the specter of the hospital monitor, a ghostly imprint hovering at the edges of his vision. The overlay flashed insistently, a grim reminder that this was more than a game, more than a raid gone awry. It taunted him with its rhythmic pulse, the real-world consequence intruding on his digital frenzy with unignorable persistence.

He thought of Julia, her voice as real in this madness as it had been beside the hospital bed. The memory of her plea cut through the digital noise, urging him back to a world that felt both distant and impossible. "I can't escape," he whispered, the words carrying the weight of despair and defiance alike.

His avatar convulsed between realities, the medieval armor he wore dissolving into the cartoon exaggeration of a racing suit. His self-glitched with each step, each swing of the sword, until it seemed that every movement might be the last. He pushed forward, a desperate determination in every pixelated stride. The sword in his hand felt heavier, less certain, and he wondered how much longer he could keep it all together.

He doubled back, launching into a counterattack against the relentless, glitching adversaries. His blade cleaved through digital ether, trailing sparks and determination, while around him, hostile code teemed with algorithmic precision. Ashlee moved with calculated desperation, seeking any opening, any chance to regroup and reorient. But the relentless forces closed in, each failure to escape knitting tighter around him like a net of luminous inevitability.

His vision swam with static, the merging realities fragmenting in earnest. The entities pressed their advantage, overwhelming and unyielding. He felt the resolution of his self-begin to falter, the pixelated world expanding to consume him entirely. He was a player without pause, without save point, and the crushing sense of inescapability loomed as large as the flashing code-driven adversaries.

One last leap, one last swing of the now-too-heavy sword, and Ashlee's form began to disintegrate in earnest. The landscape that had alternated with mocking, shifting persistence now stood still, allowing him no more avenues, no more illusion of escape. He watched, helpless, as his avatar dissolved into a stream of glowing pixels, his own presence reduced to a flickering essence.

He had just enough coherence left to wonder what it all meant, to feel the phantom throb of the heart monitor echo in a space that should have been silent. Then the digital ether claimed him entirely, leaving nothing but the pulsing residue of a vanished player.

And then, he was gone.

XIII
Rallying the Party

Decisions in the Dark

Julia stood vigil beside Ashlee's hospital bed, her gaze locked onto him with steely determination as if sheer willpower alone might tether him to the waking world. The room was cramped, thick with the sterile scent of antiseptic and the unrelenting beeps of monitors, crowding out silence. Her face softened, if only for a moment, as she reached out to touch Ashlee's hand, limp and colorless against the white sheets.

"Hang in there, Ashlee," she whispered, her voice low and fierce, more command than plea. She turned, her eyes catching Tim's just as he backed into the room, arms laden with gear.

"Right there," she said, directing him to a small, clear space on a side table.

Tim flashed a grin, unfazed by the hospital's intimidating monotony. "No worries, Julia. We'll get this set up faster than you can say 'multiplayer.'" He unpacked cables and consoles with the confidence of someone who'd done this a thousand times, quickly creating an island of familiar chaos in the sterile room.

Julia nodded, still standing rigid, but the corners of her mouth threatened a hopeful curve. "He needs this, Tim. He needs all of us."

"We're not leaving until he's back online with reality," Tim replied, giving her a reassuring pat on the shoulder.

The tangled web of wires started to resemble a makeshift gaming hub, a stark contrast to the sanitized order surrounding it. Tim, fingers working with dexterous ease, plugged in the final connection and looked up just as the tablet crackled to life.

"Ashlee, we're here with you!" Ashley's face filled the screen, bright and animated despite the digital fuzz. Her voice carried warmth and encouragement, a burst of energy cutting through the clinical setting.

"Tim, you got the console up already? I should've known!" she laughed, the sound full of life, even through the tiny speakers. "And Julia, hey! We're all rooting for Ashlee."

Julia leaned in, grateful for the cheery intrusion. "Hi, Ashley. Thanks for being here."

The image jiggled as Ashley adjusted her camera. Her red hair bobbed around her face like a living thing. "Always. We're in this together. How's Ashlee doing?" Her expression turned earnest, concern bridging the miles between them.

"Better now that he's got his team," Julia replied, letting a hint of optimism slip into her tone.

The door swung open, and Marcus walked in, a sturdy backpack over one shoulder and a smile wide enough to brighten the whole room. Fresh off a long flight, he seemed unfazed by jet lag or the solemnity of his surroundings.

"Whoa," he said, surveying the scene. "You guys look like you're prepping for an eSports tournament."

Tim threw him a mock salute. "Marcus, welcome to the party. Think we got a shot?"

Marcus dropped his bag with a thud and shot a thumbs-up to the tablet. "Ashley T! Long time, no see. I'm thinking we're about to show these games who's boss." His voice was smooth and relaxed, immediately lowering the tension.

Ashley's laugh crackled over the connection. "KnightSlayer92 in the house! Did you bring your katanas, or just that charming smile?"

He mimed pulling swords from his back. "Always both," he quipped, joining the group clustered around Ashlee's bed.

With everyone assembled, the atmosphere shifted from worry to determination. Each face turned towards Ashlee, their shared focus making the small space feel almost crowded with purpose.

Julia took a deep breath, a general rallying her troops. "We have to keep him engaged. Make sure he knows we're all right here."

"Think he can hear us?" Marcus asked, genuine curiosity in his tone.

"If not, we'll keep trying until he does," Tim said, his competitive nature surfacing. "Come on, Ashlee! Time to level up."

Ashley's voice rang out with playful enthusiasm. "We're all connected! You can't rage quit on us now!"

Julia allowed herself a small smile. "Exactly. He's not going anywhere."

The voices overlapped, lively and hopeful, creating a tapestry of support that wove through the antiseptic haze.

They strategized ways to keep Ashlee anchored, each suggestion met with nods and laughter that defied the clinical confines.

"Maybe some old-school games?" Marcus proposed, eyeing the setup. "Hit him with the nostalgia."

"And remind him of the best boss fights," Ashley chimed in, her voice insistent with belief. "He's got the best team backing him up!"

Tim snapped his fingers. "What about that multiplayer tournament he was dominating? We could remind him how much he's been owning us."

Julia's voice cut through with quiet resolve. "Whatever it takes."

They leaned in, a circle of determination around the bed, united in their mission. Tim adjusted the equipment, flipping switches that brought the setup humming to life. Marcus retrieved extra controllers, tossing them to Tim with perfect aim. Julia, ever the strategist, coordinated efforts with Ashley, the tablet sitting at Ashlee's side like a personal cheering section.

The sterile room buzzed with an energy that had nothing to do with electricity. Voices overlapped, urgent and animated, their combined efforts transforming the environment. What had been a stifling monotony became a hub of activity, a place where Ashlee's drifting presence was the only thing that seemed out of place.

"We're here for the long haul," Tim declared, a challenge in his eyes.

Marcus clapped a hand on Tim's shoulder. "Good, 'cause we need the practice."

Ashley's laughter mingled with the steady beeps. "Can't let you guys get rusty."

The group pressed closer, determined, as the flickering lights of the monitors blinked in time with their efforts. Ashlee's still form lay at the center, but with every word and every action, the room seemed to pull him closer to the edge of consciousness. Each member of this makeshift clan brought something unique: Julia's unyielding hope, Tim's infectious enthusiasm, Ashley's boundless encouragement, Marcus's calming humor.

The conversation turned from strategy to stories, anecdotes about shared games and memories that brought color to Ashlee's pale cheeks. Julia recounted the time Ashlee had single-handedly beaten an entire raid group, her tone a mix of exasperation and pride. Tim talked about the first time they'd all played together, his voice animated with fondness. Ashley added her own twist, remembering a hilarious glitch that had left them laughing for days. Marcus, grinning, recounted their latest in-game exploits, punctuating his tales with gestures that had the group in stitches.

Through it all, the monitors continued their rhythmic beeping, an indifferent metronome to the vibrant concert of human connection unfolding in that small, sterile room. Yet even that mechanical chorus seemed to fall in line, its regularity underscoring the unwavering support of Ashlee's devoted allies.

Their collective willpower filled the room, pushing against the sterile boundaries and leaving no space for doubt. Here, reality and hope met at the edge of Ashlee's consciousness, and together they stood watch, turning beeps into battle cries and antiseptic air into the breath of life.

Moments of Clarity

Ashlee materialized in a virtual realm, his digital self immediately besieged by the vivid chaos of an online battlefield. The bright colors of game worlds flashed like distant explosions, and his avatar, nimble and precise, cut through a swarm of pixelated adversaries with the expertise of someone who lived for the game. Each well-placed strike was accompanied by an echo from reality—Tim's buoyant, "Keep fighting, Ashlee!" and Ashley's infectious, "We believe in you!"—voices that guided his every move like a phantom team behind the screen.

The game settings shifted with dizzying speed. One moment, Ashlee faced a sprawling castle, his avatar's swift strikes carving a path through an army of foes. The next, he was in a dense forest, colors blurring as he dashed between digital enemies. Through it all, the swirl of action only seemed to sharpen Ashlee's focus as he pushed further into the relentless assault.

The chorus of encouragement never waned, breaking through the virtual immersion with unyielding support. "You're not alone in there!" Marcus's voice rang clear, each syllable a lifeline cast into the torrent of Ashlee's concentration. The rallying cries interwove with the vibrant chaos, turning the digital battleground into a vivid testament to friendship.

Back in the hospital, the scene briefly returned to find Julia and Marcus closely watching Ashlee, their faces a mix of concern and fierce resolve. The monitor's steady beep provided a backdrop to their low, urgent conversation.

"His fingers just twitched," Julia said, her voice a thin thread of hope. "Did you see that?"

Marcus nodded, eyes never leaving Ashlee's still form. "Yeah. He's in there. We just have to keep going."

They leaned closer, drawing strength from each other as they willed Ashlee back to consciousness. The stark room pulsed with an energy that rivaled the virtual worlds, a different kind of battlefield where love and determination stood against uncertainty.

Back in the games, the landscape shifted to a neon-lit cityscape. Ashlee moved with precision, his avatar a blur of motion as he tackled wave after wave of adversaries. His digital prowess was the result of countless hours in this realm, yet the encouragement from the real world made his strikes feel newly empowered.

Tim's voice was a steady beat amidst the chaos. "You're the MVP, man! Just like always!" His words punctuated each successful dodge and strike, a constant reminder of the support that waited outside the screen.

Ashley's enthusiastic shouts cut through the barrage of in-game sounds. "You've got this, Ashlee! We're all right here!"

With each rallying cry, Ashlee's focus seemed to sharpen, his movements more fluid and controlled. Yet beneath the unwavering skill lay a hint of struggle, a sign of his precarious tether to reality.

The hospital room's urgency matched that of the virtual worlds. Ashlee's friends stood firm, their attention never wavering as they watched for any sign of recognition. The mix of bright gaming gear and sterile medical equipment painted a unique portrait of their combined hopes.

Just then, Chen Laoshi entered with calm authority, her professional demeanor an anchor in the storm of concern. She spoke directly to the nursing staff, her voice confident and clear.

"Thank you for your care of Mr. Montgomery. We will ensure his teaching responsibilities are covered during his recovery," she said, addressing the situation with a reassuring nod. She turned to Julia, her tone softening. "It seems we have both work and games covered, yes?"

Julia let out a breath she didn't realize she'd been holding. "Chen Laoshi, I—thank you. We're trying to keep him connected."

Chen's eyes moved to the assembled group, taking in the scene with quiet understanding. "You have a good team," she observed. Her words were both a statement and a vote of confidence.

The digital battles raged on, Ashlee's avatar now in a volcanic wasteland, fire and stone creating a vivid backdrop to the melee. His movements were a blur of calculated efficiency, but with each new wave of foes, the challenges grew more intense.

Despite the onslaught, Ashlee pressed forward, every digital duel a testament to his gaming mastery. His friends' voices were a constant presence, weaving through the relentless action with unyielding belief.

"You're invincible!" Tim called, his competitive spirit translating into pure encouragement.

"Nothing can stop you!" Ashley echoed, her enthusiasm a vibrant pulse within the chaos.

But for the first time, Ashlee's avatar hesitated, a brief pause amidst the furious combat that hinted at the toll it was taking. The high-stakes duel teetered between overwhelming and triumphant, his digital self caught in a precarious dance.

Marcus looked to Julia, concern shadowing his usual smile. "We have to keep shouting until we hear him shout back."

She nodded, eyes fixed on Ashlee. "He will. I know he will."

The unwavering support seemed to reach through the digital walls, linking Ashlee's worlds with a lifeline of persistence. His avatar launched back into action, rallying with renewed vigor as his friends' determination fueled each movement.

The stakes climbed with every passing moment, a crescendo of tension that matched the rapid shifts of setting and scenario. Ashlee fought on, his real-world connection as fragile as it was vital.

The scene built to a dramatic point, each detail converging into a moment of uncertainty. The hospital's calm faced off against the virtual chaos, creating a unique duality that left Ashlee teetering between overwhelming obstacles and the urgent, hopeful chorus that demanded his return to reality.

XIV

The Boss Battle

Searching for Self

The shadows leaped like specters in the ruins, each jagged wall and shattered column alive with menace as Ashlee dove into the fray. His sword cleaved through the air, a glint of brutal beauty, striking metal and flesh with visceral finality. Sparks cascaded like tiny fireworks, illuminating the dust and blood that danced in chaotic choreography. He moved with impossible grace, an orchestrated violence born from digital realms, where instincts honed on pixelated battlefields transformed into tangible prowess. Opponents bore down, relentless in their assault, yet Ashlee twisted and spun, each evasion a masterpiece of timing and intent. Voices cut through the maelstrom, not of war but of camaraderie, threading through the clangs and shouts with intimate urgency. Julia's firm "Keep your guard up!" and Tim's infectious "You've got this, Ashlee!" rode the currents of battle, carrying his will beyond muscle and bone. Under the harsh flicker of failing torches, Ashlee fought like a hero in his own story, each fallen foe a testament to grit and the unyielding echo of belief.

The ruins spread out around him, a broken labyrinth where remnants of brutal encounters whispered their haunting tales. The air was thick with tension, a silent scream of a world abandoned to chaos. Crumbled stone and jagged steel littered the ground, turning every step into a gamble with balance and pain. Ashlee charged ahead, his form silhouetted against the harsh, shifting light. The cloak of dust around him caught the fading glow, creating an ethereal aura that spoke of legends and battles not yet written. He faced the charging group with unflinching resolve, his grip on the sword a promise of calculated destruction. As he met them, his swings spoke a language of their own, each arc and strike a word in the poetry of survival.

His world became a symphony of sensation as the clang of weapons and the grit of swirling debris painted the battlefield in stark hues of sound and touch. He felt the impact reverberate up his arms as his sword met an enemy's blade, the clash of metal a jarring melody. The taste of blood and dust was bitter on his tongue, a sharp reminder of the stakes at play. But Ashlee's body danced to an instinctive rhythm, weaving through attacks with a fluidity that seemed otherworldly. His gaming experience bled into reality, turning hesitation into action, thought into reflex. He swung his sword in a wide arc, and it hummed through the air, singing a song of precision and lethal intent.

The enemies came in waves, each one more desperate to crush him, but he parried their strikes with movements so precise they seemed preordained. His muscles tensed and released in perfect harmony, a ballet of exertion that spoke to years spent in digital conquest. They thought they could overwhelm him, a lone figure in a world collapsed under its own savagery. But they underestimated the dreamer, the one who lived where realities blurred, and every motion defied their brutal calculus. Ashlee spun, dodging an attack, and countered with a thrust that sent another opponent to the ground, the fallen body a punctuation in the narrative of his tenacity.

Julia's voice emerged like a guiding star amidst the storm, clear and unwavering. "Keep your guard up!" she called, her words slicing through the noise with a precision that mirrored Ashlee's own movements. "They won't give you a chance to breathe." The connection he felt to her transcended the physical, a lifeline of strategy and shared purpose that bolstered his resolve. Her steady presence infused him with clarity, sharpening his focus until the chaos felt almost navigable.

As the fight dragged on, Julia's encouragement became a rhythm to Ashlee's battle, a constant pulse that echoed with each heartbeat and swing. "Stay on your toes," she instructed, her tone commanding yet laced with the warmth of deep familiarity. Ashlee responded in kind, his body and spirit in tune with her guidance. He blocked an incoming strike, feeling the raw energy of battle funnel through him, turning each piece of advice into action, every suggestion into victory. Her voice was a partner in the dance of combat, pushing him to extend beyond limits he never knew he could reach.

The metallic song of blades and the raw soundtrack of conflict blended with Tim's enthusiastic shouts, bursting through the warlike anthems. "You've got this, Ashlee!" he hollered, his words igniting like fireworks against the dark sky of the melee. "Show them what you're made of!" Tim's contagious energy filled Ashlee's lungs with fresh determination, his tone vibrating with the kind of belief that turns challenges into opportunities. Ashlee's footwork grew more daring, fueled by the relentless optimism that only Tim could provide.

He lunged at his foes with renewed vigor, feeling the support of his friends morphing into a tangible force that propelled him forward. Tim's presence was a shot of adrenaline, the raw, exuberant edge that took calculated risks and transformed them into triumphant moments. "Don't let them pin you down!" Tim urged, his voice resonating with competitive fervor and unshakeable support. Ashlee ducked a high strike, Tim's words syncing with the precise timing of his evasion. He felt the exhilaration of landing critical hits, the momentum building into an unstoppable wave.

Ashley's playful banter skipped like a cheerful note over the battle's fierce chords. "Look at you go!" she laughed, her voice a bright contrast to the grim setting, yet perfectly at home in the universe Ashlee navigated. Her encouragement was infectious, sparking joy even in the heat of intense conflict. "That's the way, Ashlee!" she called, wrapping each phrase in the kind of camaraderie that knew no distance or boundary. Her laughter wove through the scene, a thread of pure, undiluted enthusiasm that pulled Ashlee toward his own sense of triumph.

He fought with a smile tugging at the corners of his mouth, feeling Ashley's warmth and belief in every sweep of his sword. Her playful spirit lifted his own, reminding him that even the most daunting challenges could be met with a light heart and fierce determination. "Make them wish they never met you!" she teased, her words an echo of shared adventures and countless battles won. Ashlee charged, buoyed by her boundless positivity, the spark she provided lighting the way through the chaos and turning grit into something luminous and powerful.

Marcus's spirited call joined the chorus, the respect of a true peer evident in every word. "Keep the pressure on, Ashlee!" he urged, the thrill of competition lacing his voice. Marcus understood the depth of Ashlee's drive, having faced him across the digital landscapes time and again. His voice was an anchor and a challenge, daring Ashlee to push even further, to become the master of this world as he had in so many others. It was the ultimate rallying cry from one dedicated gamer to another.

Ashlee responded with an intensity that matched Marcus's own, each move a testament to their shared history of rivalry and respect. He sidestepped a coordinated attack, feeling the synchronization of his body and spirit, the echo of Marcus's words turning strategy into pure instinct. "Now show them who's boss!" Marcus exclaimed, the camaraderie in his tone mixing with the competitive edge. Ashlee's strikes became more fierce, more precise, his path clear and unyielding.

Enemies that regrouped with renewed ferocity found themselves once again caught in the whirlwind of Ashlee's determination. He was unstoppable, an embodiment of focus and skill that transcended the harsh, pixelated world. The broken torches around him flickered like the fading hope of his opponents, the light growing dimmer with each swing of his sword, each victory that pushed them closer to despair. As the last adversary fell, the battlefield echoed with more than the cries of defeat. It resonated with belief, the shared, unwavering trust of friends who knew him, and knew that this was only the beginning.

Reflections of a Warrior

The colors collided in dizzying disarray, a hypercharged carnival where every hue screamed for attention as Ashlee tore down the track. Engines roared with furious abandon, a symphony of chaos that vibrated in his bones and threatened to rattle the world apart. His kart whipped around corners, wheels barely clinging to the asphalt as he launched into the electric pandemonium of the race. Rivals closed in, a blur of aggression and speed, but Ashlee danced between them, a maestro of momentum and daring. Power-ups exploded around him in violent bursts of light and sound, while hazards loomed like forgotten fears. He was lost in the tempest of color and noise, his heart a primal drum that matched the visceral thrill of the track. Ashley's exuberant "Show them how it's done!" cut through the tumult, a guiding beacon that turned frenzy into focused abandon. He surged forward, finding impossible gaps and leaving a contrail of audacious victory in his wake.

The track was a vibrant tapestry of chaos, twisting and looping in every direction. It seemed alive, a creature of boundless energy that pulsed with every screeching turn. Ashlee felt the engine's growl beneath him, a living beast that responded to his touch with eager ferocity. He gripped the wheel tightly, feeling the vibrations travel up his arms, each jolt a challenge, each lurch a promise of more. As he tore into the first bend, the world blurred, the scenery a whirlpool of primary colors that enveloped him in its dizzying embrace. He was part of the track, one with its wild rhythm and furious pace.

Enemy karts closed in, a relentless swarm of competition and danger. They jockeyed for position, metal shells bristling with intent as they aimed to box him in and cut him off. Ashlee could see the determination etched in the lines of their speeding forms, but he wouldn't be trapped so easily. His fingers danced on the controls, coaxing more speed, more daring from the machine beneath him. He zigged and zagged, defying the lines they tried to draw around him, his kart a blur of defiance as he slipped through their nets and gained the lead.

Power-ups and hazards became a minefield of possibilities, each one an opportunity or a threat. Explosive items detonated around him, their force a visceral kick that rattled his senses. Ashlee wove through the chaos, his timing impeccable as he skirted danger with millimeters to spare. The world exploded in flashes of light and sound, an overwhelming feast of the senses that threatened to consume him. Yet within the pandemonium, Ashlee found his groove, a dance with the track that felt both new and achingly familiar.

The race's unrelenting pace quickened his pulse, each lap a sprint that pushed him further into the heart of exhilaration. He felt alive, every nerve and muscle attuned to the wild pulse of the track. Adrenaline surged through him, turning doubt into daring, caution into thrill. The memory of the earlier battle faded into the background, its grim intensity replaced by the vibrant clamor of the race. He was in the moment, a streak of color and resolve, the joy of speed propelling him forward.

Ashley's voice rang out again, a burst of exuberant encouragement that cut through the roar. "That's how you do it!" she cheered, her laughter bright and infectious, the perfect harmony to the chaos of the track. Her words wrapped around him like a charged boost, lifting his spirits and renewing his resolve. "Keep it up, Ashlee!" she called, turning the frenzy into a game, a challenge that spoke to every competitive bone in his body.

He responded with a flair that matched her enthusiasm, executing moves that seemed impossible, yet felt right. He darted between rival karts, threading the needle with the finesse of a seasoned racer. Ashlee found lines and gaps that defied logic, his instincts guiding him through the tempest of speed and sound. He felt the wind rushing past, a fierce caress that spoke of freedom and abandon. Ashley's presence was a constant, joyful echo, a reminder that even amidst chaos, fun was the ultimate victory.

The race intensified, the track throwing more obstacles, more chaos in his path. Each lap escalated the challenge, turning up the volume on speed and risk. Ashlee remained undeterred, his confidence growing with each close call, each successful dodge. He was the architect of his own audacity, the creator of a narrative where only he decided the outcome. The world spun around him in glorious disarray, the pulse of the race his constant companion.

Every second crackled with electricity, every movement charged with purpose. The smell of burning rubber filled the air, mingling with the sweet, fierce scent of adrenaline and resolve. Ashlee embraced the chaos, wearing it like a second skin as he tore through the heart of the race. The challenges felt infinite, the possibilities endless, a testament to his refusal to yield to anything less than victory.

Julia's steady voice joined the chorus, bringing strategy and focus to the swirling madness. "Watch those turns, Ashlee," she advised, her words a cool balm that cut through the frenetic heat. "You've got the lead. Keep it." Her presence was grounding, a thread of calm determination amidst the unrestrained thrill. Her guidance spoke of balance, the perfect complement to the wild ride Ashlee was on.

Tim's enthusiastic shout followed, his voice a spark that set the air alight. "Catch that drift, Ashlee!" he exclaimed, his tone bursting with excitement. "Don't let them catch you!" His belief was as unwavering as his friendship, a booster that propelled Ashlee to even greater speeds. With every turn and swerve, Ashlee felt their voices propel him forward, weaving through the chaos with a unity that transcended distance and doubt.

The final stretch loomed ahead, a tunnel of speed and possibility that beckoned like a siren. Ashlee leaned into it, his heart a furious drum that matched the primal tempo of the track. It was the pure essence of race and resolve, a crucible where skill met the relentless pursuit of thrill. His kart surged forward, a streak of audacious defiance that left a charged, electrifying wake behind. Ashlee tore through the finish with a victory born not just of speed, but of the shared spirit that had carried him to the very edge.

Rhythms of the Arena

Ashlee stood on the edge of a battle so alive with color and sound it seemed to pulse with its own frantic heartbeat. The stage morphed and shifted beneath him, platforms gliding like celestial bodies across the riotous sky. Explosive energy raced between combatants, each projectile a wild declaration of intent. His body responded with instinctual agility, honed by the worlds he had conquered before, turning every leap and dodge into a calculated waltz of strategy and speed. He moved like quicksilver, precise and elusive, his attacks a flurry of well-placed strikes that played his opponents like instruments in a cacophonous symphony. They jeered and taunted, but Ashlee's focused rhythm drowned them out, a counterpoint of determination and skill. Marcus's spirited

"Keep the pressure on, Ashlee!" wove through the frenetic landscape, transforming the stage from chaos into a realm of deliberate and artful conflict.

The stage was a living, breathing thing, a vibrant organism that defied stasis and expectation. Platforms shifted with a will of their own, offering fleeting sanctuaries that promised safety only to snatch it away. They floated and spun, a constellation of opportunity and risk that redefined the battlefield with every second. Ashlee stood amidst the riot, his form silhouetted against the dazzling tapestry of combat. It was chaos, it was beauty, and it called to every part of him that had ever lived for the thrill of the game.

Enemies crowded the stage, their animated forms a swirl of bravado and intent. They closed in, attacking with the abandon of those who knew they had nothing to lose. Ashlee felt the barrage of projectiles whizz past, each one a statement of defiance. Yet he moved with a finesse that seemed to defy the very laws they tried to impose, a physical poetry that left them grasping at empty air. He leaped between platforms with effortless grace, his every movement an exercise in adaptability and foresight.

Taunts echoed through the arena, a soundtrack of derision and challenge that sought to undermine his focus. "Get him!" they cried, their voices an aggressive crescendo. "You're not going to last!" But Ashlee was a veteran of such contests, his mental armor as fortified as the reflexes he displayed. The chaos became his ally, the noise a familiar companion that whispered strategies rather than distractions. He tuned out the jeers, allowing his instincts to lead him in a dance that was as much about evasion as it was about attack.

His counterattacks were precise, a symphony of movement that spoke of time well spent in worlds like this. Ashlee's strikes landed with uncanny accuracy, sending foes flying in wide arcs, their surprise a silent homage to his skill. He launched a rapid combo, the speed and fluidity of his assault a stark contrast to their faltering defenses. Each hit was a note in the larger composition of his strategy, a crescendo that sent yet another opponent staggering from the stage.

Marcus's voice cut through the explosive clamor, a beacon of camaraderie and shared ambition. "Keep the pressure on, Ashlee!" he called, his words infusing the battle with a new intensity. Marcus's encouragement was like an energy boost, turning Ashlee's steady rhythm into something more, something unstoppable. It was the voice of a fellow player who understood the stakes and shared in the triumphs, the perfect counterbalance to the taunts and distractions of his enemies.

Ashlee responded to Marcus's shout with a flurry of attacks that spoke to his adaptability and resolve. He knew this game, knew it on a level that transcended mere mechanics. It was part of him, as natural as breathing, as essential as the victory he chased. The rapid exchanges escalated in intensity, each dodge and strike a testament to the connection he felt to the arena, to the fight, to the very act of gaming itself.

His tactics evolved with the battlefield, each change in strategy a response to the ever-shifting stage. Ashlee's movements were fluid, his thought process a stream of constant recalibration. He anticipated their attacks, saw their strategies before they did, turning their attempts to outsmart him into opportunities for devastating counterplay. It was the art of the adaptive gamer, the hallmark of someone who lived for the challenge and the satisfaction of overcoming it.

Skill and tenacity blended into a singular, driving force, an essence that defined Ashlee's approach to the game and to the stage itself. The vibrant chaos of the battlefield became his canvas, and he painted it with the broad strokes of determination and the fine lines of expertise. His opponents seemed to falter, their initial confidence shaken by the relentlessness of his offense and the unpredictability of his defense. Ashlee fought with the heart of a true competitor, refusing to cede any ground, any momentum.

As the battle reached its fever pitch, Ashlee found his rhythm, an unstoppable cadence that saw him dominating the stage. He moved with an unerring sense of purpose, an artist in a world of vivid, kinetic action, where every platform and projectile was both obstacle and inspiration. The arena was alive, a brilliant symphony of motion and color that echoed with the certainty of his victory. Ashlee's mastery of the chaotic stage was complete, and as the final opponents fell, the sound of triumph filled the space, reverberating with the certainty that he was ready for whatever came next.

Fractured Mindscape

The world fragmented and reassembled, a mindscape as intricate as Ashlee's own thoughts, where chaos was both the architecture and the artist. Elements from ruined battles, furious races, and strategic arenas converged in a breathtaking symphony of disorder, a dreamscape that defied logic and expectation. Ashlee stood at the epicenter, confronting a monstrous avatar of his own self-doubt, a fearsome creature forged from every challenge he faced and every insecurity that lingered. It roared with the fury of racing engines and the clamor of endless battles, a daunting synthesis of the worlds he'd conquered and the one that loomed within. But he moved with purpose, the avatars of armor and energy unable to crush the resolve he'd honed. Voices of friendship and belief twined through the surreal vista, creating a harmonious chorus that steadied him: Julia's firm, "Don't let fear stop you," Tim's energetic, "You're stronger than this," Ashley's assuring, "Every move counts," and Marcus's resolute, "Now finish it!" Ashlee advanced through the kaleidoscope of color and sound, each step a confrontation with the specter of doubt, each swing a proclamation of resilience. As the realm reached the height of its shifting, surreal splendor, Ashlee readied for the final blow, a strike poised to redefine more than the battlefield.

The mindscape spread out in breathtaking chaos, an elaborate tapestry of Ashlee's inner world that sprawled beyond the borders of reason. Sections of battle-worn ruins rose from the ground, spectral echoes of past conflicts. They melded with the bright, twisting loops of race tracks, turning into an Escher-like architecture of loops and walls that defied gravity and logic. Platforms hovered in between, an impossible suspension of realities that spoke to the uncharted territories of his mind. Each element clashed and harmonized in turn, a symphonic chaos that matched the furious pace of Ashlee's thoughts and doubts.

In the heart of this surreal landscape stood the creature, a monstrous embodiment of every fear and hesitation Ashlee had ever faced. It towered over the fractured realm, a nightmarish fusion of brutal armor and screaming engines. Energy blasts radiated from its core, wild and untamed, a stark representation of chaos and challenge. It was fear given form, the collective weight of self-doubt turned into an adversary of titanic proportions. Yet, as it loomed and roared, Ashlee felt not the chill of intimidation but the familiar fire of determination.

The creature lunged with ferocious intent, its massive limbs and destructive projectiles a testament to the obstacles Ashlee knew too well. Armor clanged like battlefield echoes, karts sped with the dizzying roar of adrenaline, and energy bursts flew in erratic, blinding arcs. But Ashlee had prepared for this moment, in ways he only now began to understand. He met the creature's onslaught with a deftness honed across countless encounters, both virtual and real, where doubts were monsters of a different kind. His muscles tensed with resolve, his instincts singing the familiar tunes of challenge and triumph.

He fought back with a calculated ferocity, each strike and dodge more than just physical actions—they were declarations of the self-belief he'd crafted through persistence and passion. The chaos of the realm could not unsettle him, not now, not when it had become his natural state, his creative playground. Ashlee moved with fluid purpose, his attacks deliberate and sharp, each swing of his sword an answer to the doubts that had haunted him. The surreal world blurred around him, but his focus remained crystal clear.

Julia's voice emerged through the pandemonium, a clarion call of clarity that cut through the tumultuous air. "Don't let fear stop you," she urged, her words like a guiding hand through the uncertainty. Her tone was steadfast, unwavering, the perfect antidote to the clamor of the mindscape. Her belief became his own, a shared certainty that fortified his spirit and sharpened his will. It was a strategic brilliance that spoke of her deep understanding, both of the battle at hand and the battles Ashlee waged within.

Her encouragement transformed the frenetic chaos into a manageable series of challenges, turning doubt into a puzzle Ashlee was determined to solve. He felt the boost her presence gave him, a direct line of purpose and determination that cleared a path through the cacophony of colors and fears. With every dodge and counterattack, her words became a part of his core, a steady rhythm that fueled his resistance against the looming, monstrous specter.

Tim's energetic voice followed, a bolt of enthusiasm that crackled with potential. "You're stronger than this!" he shouted, his exuberance infusing the very air with vitality. Tim's belief in Ashlee was palpable, a dynamic force that sparked new life into each of Ashlee's actions. The engine of doubt could not outrun the speed of conviction that Tim imparted, the powerful belief that Ashlee was capable of conquering not just games but the deeper challenges they mirrored.

Ashlee felt his confidence grow with each heartbeat, a steady crescendo that matched the escalating tempo of the surreal encounter. Tim's words were adrenaline in verbal form, charging his limbs and spirit with the courage to face this ultimate test. The rapid rhythm of the battle transformed into a dance of freedom, where Ashlee's movements were unhindered by the constraints of hesitation or fear. He pushed forward, every step a bold testament to the strength that Tim's encouragement revealed in him.

Ashley joined the symphony of support, her voice a melody of assurance that wound through the fractured landscape with unwavering warmth. "Every move counts!" she encouraged, her words a playful reminder that resonated with more than just the competitive heart of the challenge. Her presence was like a lifeline, a connection that bridged the gap between isolation and community, reminding Ashlee that he was never alone in this battle or any other.

With Ashley's laughter echoing in his mind, the fight became less about survival and more about embracing the full, unrestrained scope of possibility. He swung with joyful defiance, feeling the energy of their shared experiences infuse each calculated move. Her encouragement was the bright beacon that turned the dark specter of doubt into an opponent he could—and would—conquer. It was a game, it was a challenge, and above all, it was a story he was writing with every determined strike.

Marcus's shout broke through like a rallying cry from the heart of the battlefield, resolute and confident. "Now finish it!" he declared, his words a direct challenge that transformed into the ultimate encouragement. Marcus knew Ashlee's capabilities, knew them from countless matches and rivalries, and his call to arms resonated with a trust that transcended even the surreal madness of the scene. It was the challenge of a peer, the confidence of a friend who knew the depth of Ashlee's tenacity.

The fight reached its most vivid, intense crescendo as Ashlee embraced Marcus's call, surging with unyielding momentum towards the monstrous avatar of doubt. The elements of color and sound, once chaotic, aligned in perfect, surreal harmony around him. His friends' voices melded into a single, powerful anthem of belief and determination. Ashlee's world, once fractured and intimidating, transformed into a coherent expression of his resolve, each texture and hue a testament to his refusal to yield.

In the height of the clash, with the surreal landscape swirling in breathtaking disorder and certainty, Ashlee prepared to deliver the decisive blow. It was a moment that transcended the battlefield, a strike poised to redefine more than just the game world. It was a confrontation with self, a declaration of identity, an unwavering stand against the fears and doubts that sought to claim him. Ashlee's strike cut through the chaos with brilliant clarity, and as the realm teetered on the brink of possibility, the outcome hung suspended, a promise of victory and the untold stories yet to unfold.

XV
Awakening

Clashing Worlds

The first thing Ashlee noticed was the antiseptic smell, sharper than any sword he'd wielded in the virtual world. The sterile light of the hospital room blinked him into consciousness, while the steady beeping of monitors composed an unwelcome but reassuring soundtrack. Julia was there, a pillar of tense relief as she leaned close to him. Tim stood nearby, the corners of his mouth turning up in a supportive grin. Marcus leaned against the wall with furrowed concentration, arms crossed as if preparing for another boss fight. Chen Laoshi flipped through a chart with crisp efficiency, and Ashley's face appeared, flickering with anxious pixels on a tablet mounted to the bed.

"I'm so glad you're back," Julia said softly, as the hum of machines filled the room with ambient reassurance.

Tim chimed in, "We worried about you, man," his voice mingling with the electronic symphony.

Ashlee struggled to sit up, groaning as his body resisted, every detail sharpening the reality of the moment. The wrinkle of worry on Marcus's forehead, Chen Laoshi's nod,

Ashley's bright, curious eyes—all of it reminded him how much these tangible connections mattered, how much they anchored him more than any digital escape.

Julia reached to help him, her hand warm and firm. "Take it easy," she urged. Her eyes held a mix of concern and relief.

"You had us in a bit of a panic," Tim added, stepping closer. The half-smile on his face didn't quite hide his anxiety.

Ashlee tried to piece together how he'd ended up here. The last thing he remembered was an intense battle in Elden Ring, facing off against an enemy that had taken on monstrous proportions. But now, the muted colors of the hospital room were replacing the vivid hues of the game world.

He settled back against the pillows, feeling their scratchy texture. "How long was I out?"

"A couple of hours," Marcus replied, his voice steady but edged with tension. "You really scared us, Ashlee."

Chen Laoshi gave a small, reassuring nod. "The doctors say you are recovering well. But it seems you've been living quite an adventurous life lately."

The reality of their presence wrapped around him like a safety net, pulling him further from the virtual cliffs he'd been hanging off of. "Guess I should have leveled up my stamina in real life," he mumbled, a weak smile creeping onto his face.

Tim chuckled, more relieved than amused. "You were way off script, man. We were about to do a rescue mission IRL."

Ashlee tried to sit up again, wincing at the stiffness in his limbs. Tim quickly moved to support him, the mattress shifting under Ashlee's weight as he settled into a more upright position.

"You all look like you've seen a ghost," Ashlee said, the lightness of his words failing to hide his own unease.

"We almost did," Julia replied, her voice a careful blend of sternness and warmth.

Marcus shifted, the cross of his arms loosening as he joined the conversation. "It's like you were in another world, Ashlee. Seriously."

Chen Laoshi pushed her glasses atop her head and added, "Perhaps now is the time to rethink your gaming career."

Ashlee watched them, his circle of friends, their care weaving through the sterile air more effectively than any treatment could. "I didn't think it was that bad," he confessed, his gaze dropping to where Julia's hand held his.

Tim squeezed his shoulder with friendly force. "You were playing like your life depended on it, man. Almost gave us a heart attack."

The tension in the room began to unravel, replaced by a lighter energy as they realized he was genuinely back with them. Ashlee felt a rush of gratitude that was more overwhelming than any victory screen.

Ashley's voice came through the tablet, crackling with digital warmth. "You're like a real-life hero now, Ashlee! How's it feel? xD"

The absurdity of the question made him laugh, and the sound was like a balm to the assembled crew. Even Chen Laoshi cracked a smile.

"Exhausting," Ashlee admitted. He looked around at each of them, their concerned expressions softening. Julia, with her determined gaze, showing the depth of her love beneath that composed exterior. Tim, all exuberant worry and good-natured relief. Marcus, competitive spirit muted by genuine concern. Chen Laoshi, offering structured reassurance. And Ashley, a flickering beacon of enthusiasm on a screen, as vibrant as ever.

The noises of the hospital faded into the background as Ashlee let himself truly appreciate the people around him. He'd spent so long immersed in his games, crafting connections in virtual worlds, but none of it matched the impact of these real, breathing relationships.

He took a deep breath, the antiseptic air filling his lungs. It felt like a new beginning. "Thanks for being here, everyone. I mean it."

Julia gave his hand a gentle squeeze, locking eyes with him in a silent promise that they'd find a way forward together. Marcus nodded, more serious than Ashlee had ever seen him, and Tim offered another shoulder squeeze.

"We're just glad you're back in the game that really matters," Tim said, the joke failing to mask the sincerity of his words.

The first chapter of Ashlee's new reality had begun, written in the lines of worry and relief etched into the faces of those who cared about him most.

When Fire Meets Ice

They gathered around Ashlee's bed like characters from a beloved campaign, eager to hear the next installment of the epic they'd only glimpsed the end of. His voice wavered at first, uneven and unsure, as he recounted the battles he'd lived inside his mind. "Sometimes I couldn't tell where the game stopped and I began," he admitted, the surreal merging of fantasy and reality still fresh in his memory.

Tim chuckled, shaking his head in incredulous admiration. "You really took gaming to a whole new level, didn't you?"

Julia sat beside Ashlee, her expression a mix of determination and relief as she squeezed his hand. "We need to make changes, Ashlee. I can't keep watching you drift away into these dreams."

Marcus nodded along, more somber than Ashlee had ever seen him. Chen Laoshi, clipboard in hand, echoed the group's concern. "How do we bridge this gap between what's real and what you experienced?"

In the charged silence, Ashley's voice came through the tablet with unwavering warmth, reassuring him, "We're all here for you." And just like that, it was settled—a new quest to reshape their life together and keep Ashlee grounded in a reality where the most impressive level was the one they would build side by side.

Ashlee leaned back against the pillows, his body tired but his spirit renewed by their support. He felt a swirl of gratitude and vulnerability. "I was fighting this crazy boss," he started, meeting their expectant eyes, "and suddenly I felt like I was inside the game. Like it wasn't pixels but real flesh and blood."

Tim raised an eyebrow, grinning. "You were in the zone, man, but you gotta give us the cheat code next time."

Ashlee laughed softly, though he knew Tim's words held a serious undertone. "It got pretty intense. One second I was dodging digital swords, and the next, it felt like my whole life was on the line."

Julia listened intently, her grip on his hand tightening as if to anchor him. "Ashlee, I can't tell you how relieved I am that you're okay. But we really need to talk about this obsession."

Her voice was firm yet tender, and Ashlee felt the full weight of her concern. He realized how much his gaming had affected her, how it had pulled him away from the real world they shared.

Marcus spoke up, his usual competitive banter replaced by sincerity. "We don't want to lose you to a fantasy world, Ashlee. You're too important to us."

His words echoed through the room, reaching Ashlee with a force he hadn't expected. He nodded, overwhelmed by their collective care.

Chen Laoshi adjusted her glasses and addressed Ashlee with thoughtful precision. "It seems we need a strategy. How do we keep your passion without letting it consume you?"

Ashlee appreciated her directness, the way she approached the situation like a complex problem to be solved. It made the task ahead feel more manageable.

Ashley's voice filled the silence, bright and encouraging. "Whatever you need, we're all here. This is like an epic quest, and we've got your back! :D"

The room was filled with a sense of unity, each friend bringing their unique strengths to the challenge. Ashlee looked at their faces, their presence more vivid and comforting than any game world he'd known.

He took a deep breath, feeling the steady rhythm of reality. "It means a lot, you all being here. I don't know how to thank you."

Julia gave him a knowing look, her eyes softening. "Stay with us, Ashlee. That's thanks enough."

The truth of her words settled over him, and he felt a renewed determination to stay grounded, to cherish the world they were building together.

They spent the next hour talking about practical ways to keep him connected to reality, brainstorming with the same intensity they might have planned a co-op mission. Tim suggested regular hangouts to balance screen time.

Marcus offered to keep him in check with scheduled game nights, promising more serious rematches. Chen Laoshi proposed a structured approach, suggesting time limits and physical activities. Ashley volunteered virtual support, cheering him on with her usual enthusiasm.

Ashlee absorbed their ideas, feeling more hopeful with each suggestion. The plans took shape, tangible and reassuring. He realized this was the greatest adventure he could embark on, surrounded by people who cared.

Julia sat close, watching him with a mix of relief and affection. Ashlee knew there would be challenges, but the promise in her eyes made him believe they could conquer anything together.

The room was alive with their resolve, the hum of machines a quiet backdrop to the stronger rhythm of friendship and love. As they wrapped up, Ashlee felt lighter, more anchored in the present than he'd been in a long time.

"Let's do this," he said, meeting each of their eyes in turn. The shared commitment filled the room, a collective vow that this was only the beginning of a new, shared quest.

XVI
Resetting the Game

Judgement in the Digital Arena

Ashlee opened the door to his freshly organized apartment, casting off the workday along with his jacket. The comforting aroma of green tea and the sight of Julia in the kitchenette met him like a warm embrace. "I need you here, with me," she said, her tone loving but clear, holding a steaming mug that underscored her resolve. He nodded, a quiet agreement to rebuild the balance in their lives, as the steady hum of the refrigerator and clink of utensils created a soft symphony of home.

"You've really streamlined this place," Ashlee remarked, glancing around at the tidy living space. "I barely recognize it."

Julia's smile was gentle, but there was an edge of seriousness in her eyes. "I thought it might help us both feel more... settled."

Ashlee took a deep breath, letting the scent of tea and reassurance wash over him. He understood the layers in her words.

"Sit with me?" she invited, moving to the small table by the window.

Ashlee joined her, appreciating the way her long, dark hair framed her determined gaze. "You've been incredibly patient with me, you know."

She reached for his hand, her touch warm. "I want us to have something real, Ashlee. Something we're both present for."

He squeezed her fingers lightly. "I know I've been AFK a lot lately. It's just…" He hesitated, searching for the right words. "Those games—they pull me in."

"And I love that about you," she said, her tone softening. "But I need to know we're building something here, together."

He nodded, a sense of relief mingling with resolve. "I can dial back. We can make a schedule, something that respects us both."

Julia's expression relaxed, her confidence shifting to gratitude. "I'd like that. I'd like that a lot."

The refrigerator hummed in agreement, the soft sounds of domesticity filling the room as Ashlee and Julia found a rhythm in their conversation.

Julia reached for a notepad and pen, setting them between herself and Ashlee. "Let's put something down in writing," she suggested, a twinkle of playfulness in her eyes.

"Contract binding, huh?" Ashlee teased, picking up the pen.

"Only if it's written in blue ink," Julia quipped back, her smile breaking into laughter.

He clicked the pen and began to write, his handwriting as precise and thoughtful as his words. "Let's see… Monday nights, game night with Tim and the crew. Thursdays, focus time for lesson planning."

"And Tuesday, Wednesday, and Friday, with me?" she prompted, adding a little musical flourish to her question.

"Absolutely," Ashlee replied, nodding as he jotted down her suggestions. "All other time, party of two."

Julia's eyes danced with warmth as she added a small heart next to her initial, marking her agreement. The weight of uncertainty seemed to lift, leaving behind the lightness of renewed understanding.

"It's nice to see you this way," she said, her voice colored with affection. "I've missed it."

Ashlee paused, feeling the truth of her words. "I've missed it too. More than I realized."

They sat in companionable silence for a moment, each absorbing the new promises that were being made. The steam from Julia's tea curled into the air, mingling with the feeling of hopefulness that had settled around them.

He looked up, his brown hair falling slightly over one eye. "Thanks for sticking with me, Julia."

She reached across the table, touching his arm. "We're a team, Ashlee. That's what this is all about."

"Even when my respawn time is way too long?"

"Even then," she assured him, her voice full of warmth and sincerity.

Ashlee placed the notepad in the center of the table, as if solidifying their shared commitment. He looked around the apartment again, this time seeing not just order but the intention behind it.

"I think we're gonna be just fine," he said, pushing back his chair.

Julia stood with him, her presence as grounding as the earth-toned decor she'd chosen. "It's a start."

Together, they moved from the table, a renewed sense of connection apparent in every glance and gesture.

"Want to pick out a movie for later?" Ashlee offered, pausing as he passed the small shelf of DVDs.

"You pick," Julia said. "As long as it's not one of those three-hour epics."

"Deal," Ashlee replied, heading towards the living room with a playful salute.

His steps carried him with new purpose, a tangible promise echoing in the air behind him. Julia watched him go, her heart lightened by the sense of balance they were reclaiming together.

Repercussions in Reality

Ashlee stood at the front of his classroom, a lively arena filled with students ready to tackle their latest quest. With the digital whiteboard illuminating his lessons, he moved through examples as fluidly as a boss fight, bringing his teaching to life. Chen Laoshi observed from the back, her approval as clear as Ashlee's voice, which resonated with enthusiasm and clarity.

"Alright, team," Ashlee began, leaning against his desk with an inviting posture. "Today's mission is teamwork and problem-solving. Who's ready to level up?"

Hands shot up, and Ashlee chuckled. "Thought so. Let's jump into it!"

He tapped the screen, and the board displayed a vibrant array of puzzles and challenges. His students' eyes widened with excitement.

"Think of each problem as a mini boss fight," Ashlee explained. "Every challenge has a weakness. Your job is to find it."

His confident gestures and warm tone made even the most complex tasks seem approachable. Students exchanged eager glances, and a ripple of animated whispers filled the room.

Chen Laoshi, standing at the back, nodded with a smile. Her presence lent Ashlee an extra boost of confidence as he continued his energetic presentation.

"Remember, communication is key," he said, moving to the other side of the room. "You wouldn't rush into a raid without talking to your team, right?"

A few students laughed, while others nodded seriously. Ashlee was in his element, using metaphors that bridged the gap between gaming and academics.

He paused for a moment, scanning the room. "Okay, let's strategize," he called, clapping his hands together. "What's our first move?"

A student in the front raised his hand. "Work together to identify the problem?" he suggested.

"Exactly!" Ashlee responded, pointing at the boy like a seasoned coach. "Start with the big picture, then focus on smaller tasks."

He clicked to the next slide, illustrating his point with a colorful diagram. The students leaned forward, drawn into his clear and relatable narrative.

"Think of this as your map," Ashlee continued. "It's like charting a course in a new game world. Who doesn't love exploring?"

More laughter filled the room, and Ashlee's smile broadened. He could feel the energy building, his approach connecting with the young minds before him.

"Let's split into groups," he directed. "Work through these challenges, and remember—sharing your ideas is like sharing loot. Everyone benefits!"

The students eagerly formed teams, diving into the material with enthusiasm. The room buzzed with focused chatter, the sound of young minds engaging fully with the tasks at hand.

Ashlee moved among them, offering tips and encouragement. His demeanor was supportive yet laid-back, allowing the students to discover solutions on their own.

"Think outside the box," he advised one group, gesturing to their worksheet. "Sometimes the best strategy is the one no one expects."

As they contemplated his advice, Ashlee glanced back at Chen Laoshi. She watched with keen interest, her expressions showing both pride and amusement.

He returned to the front of the class, tapping the board to highlight a particularly tricky question. "Let's regroup for a second. What do you think? Have you found the weak spot yet?"

A chorus of voices offered different strategies, and Ashlee listened with genuine interest. "All great ideas," he said, nodding approvingly. "Keep experimenting. There's always more than one way to win."

The interactive session continued with spirited exchanges and thoughtful problem-solving. Ashlee's teaching style transformed the classroom into a dynamic environment where creativity and collaboration thrived.

His use of humor kept the atmosphere light, while his clear communication ensured that students stayed on track. "Remember," he reminded them, "mistakes are just extra lives. Use them to learn!"

As the class drew to a close, the energy in the room remained high. Students wrapped up their activities, and Ashlee called for their attention once more.

"Fantastic work, everyone," he said, beaming with pride. "You've really conquered those challenges."

Chen Laoshi made her way to the front, adding her own words of praise. "Ashlee's strategies seem to be working well," she commented, her voice warm and approving. "Perhaps we'll have to send him on more quests like this."

The students laughed, and Ashlee felt a surge of accomplishment. He had turned an ordinary lesson into an extraordinary experience, blending his passion for gaming with his dedication to teaching.

As the bell rang, the class reluctantly gathered their things, already chatting about the next session. Chen Laoshi gave Ashlee a satisfied pat on the shoulder, signaling her appreciation for his innovative approach.

"Well done, Ashlee," she said, her words simple but sincere. "Very well done."

He watched the students file out, their enthusiasm echoing in the now-quiet room. A sense of fulfillment settled over him, and he took a moment to reflect on how far he'd come in balancing his worlds.

Game on

The glow of Ashlee's laptop cast playful shadows around the living room as he settled in for a gaming session with Tim, Ashley, and Marcus. Their laughter and teasing remarks bounced through the speakers, creating a virtual hangout that felt as real as any in-person meet-up. Ashlee's posture was relaxed, the new balance in his life evident as their friendly voices filled the air.

"Montgomery, you in?" Tim's voice came through with a competitive edge, his excitement palpable even over the connection.

"Here and ready," Ashlee replied, adjusting his headphones. "No cheat codes this time, right?"

"Only if you share them!" Tim shot back, chuckling.

Ashley chimed in with her trademark enthusiasm. "Oh, it's gonna be epic. We've got the dream team tonight!"

Marcus's voice followed, smooth and confident. "Game on! Hope you've all been practicing. :P"

Ashlee grinned at their familiar banter, feeling the warm camaraderie of his gaming circle. The digital world opened before them, inviting and full of possibilities.

"What's our strategy?" Ashley asked, her tone bright and eager.

Tim jumped in quickly. "I say we rush the objective. Hit it hard and fast."

Marcus countered with a playful challenge. "And give them an easy win? Let's go stealth and catch them off guard."

Ashlee leaned forward, fingers hovering over the keys. "How about we improvise? Mix it up and keep them guessing."

The team agreed, and they launched into the session, their characters moving seamlessly through the virtual landscape. Ashlee's avatar darted with precision, his focus sharp yet relaxed.

They navigated through obstacles and opponents, their voices creating a lively soundtrack to the intense but friendly competition.

"Cover me, Ashley!" Marcus called, his words turning into a laugh as a near miss flashed on the screen.

"On it!" she replied, quick and supportive. "And I thought you were the pro!"

"Only on weekends," Marcus admitted with a grin in his voice.

The action was fast-paced, each player bringing their unique style and humor to the game. Ashlee's earlier tension melted away, replaced by a sense of joy and connection.

"Nice save, Ashlee," Tim said, a note of admiration sneaking through his usual ribbing. "You're not holding back tonight."

Ashlee's avatar executed a swift move, and he chuckled. "All in good fun, right?"

They continued the challenge, celebrating small victories and recovering quickly from their occasional defeats. The game was as much about the shared experience as the outcome, a testament to their close-knit group.

"Keep it up, team!" Ashley encouraged, her energy contagious. "We've got this!"

The glow of the screen lit up Ashlee's face, the rhythmic clicking of keys and controllers adding to the cozy ambiance. He was fully immersed yet entirely at ease, embodying the balance he'd promised to Julia.

The real-time action unfolded with thrilling unpredictability, and the team's camaraderie shone through every playful taunt and cheer of triumph.

"Watch out for the trap!" Marcus warned, just in time for a skillful maneuver by Tim.

"Think we didn't see that coming?" Tim replied, quick to counter.

Their voices mixed with the sound effects, creating an atmosphere as rich and engaging as the game itself. The session continued with spirited exchanges and well-timed teamwork.

They neared the end of the match, their coordination smooth and effective. The final moments were filled with intense concentration, followed by collective celebration.

"GG, everyone!" Marcus exclaimed. "Well played."

"Yeah, that was awesome!" Ashley added. "We make a pretty good squad."

Ashlee leaned back, a satisfied smile on his face. "Not bad for a bunch of noobs," he teased gently.

The session wrapped up with promises of another game soon, the warmth of their connection lingering even as the chat faded.

"Same time next week?" Tim proposed, always eager for the next round.

"I'm in," Ashlee said, feeling the fulfillment of an evening well spent.

"Wouldn't miss it," Ashley affirmed, her laugh echoing like a cheerful punctuation.

"xD," Marcus typed, his old-school gaming charm ever-present.

Ashlee closed his laptop, the soft light of the room settling around him like a comforting blanket. He sat for a moment, savoring the blend of digital excitement and real-life balance.

The room was quiet again, but the echoes of friendship and fun remained, leaving him content and ready for whatever adventure came next.

Confronting the Inner Abyss

The softly lit office exuded calm, with potted plants and serene artworks creating an inviting sanctuary. Ashlee sat across from his therapist, his posture attentive as he recounted his day's challenges and small victories. The air was light with the scent of freshly brewed tea, mirroring the constructive tone of their session.

"It's been a week of interesting quests," Ashlee said, a hint of humor in his voice. He relaxed into his chair, feeling the space around him encourage openness.

The therapist nodded, her demeanor both professional and welcoming. "Tell me about them," she prompted gently.

Ashlee glanced at the tasteful decor, appreciating how even the setting seemed to encourage thoughtful reflection. "Things are really coming together at home. Julia and I mapped out a schedule, and it's actually working."

The therapist smiled, noting something on her clipboard. "That's wonderful to hear. How do you think that's been possible?"

He took a moment to consider. "I guess it's like… setting a game plan. We made sure it was something we both agreed on. Something realistic."

The therapist leaned slightly forward, her interest genuine. "And how does that feel?"

"Solid," Ashlee replied, his tone clear and certain. "Like I'm finally hitting the right balance between gaming and real life."

Their conversation flowed with an easy rhythm, Ashlee's introspection unfolding naturally under the therapist's attentive guidance.

"What about your work?" she inquired. "Are you finding the same success there?"

Ashlee's expression brightened, recalling the vibrant energy of his classroom. "Absolutely. I'm using gaming strategies to teach teamwork and problem-solving. The students are really engaged."

He explained how he related complex challenges to battle scenarios, turning lessons into interactive quests that the students were eager to tackle. "Think of each test question as a mini boss," he'd told them, drawing laughter and understanding in equal measure.

The therapist listened intently, her expression thoughtful. "It sounds like you've found a way to bring your passions together."

Ashlee nodded, the connection clear in his mind. "I have. And it's not just about games; it's about the skills they teach. Teamwork, persistence, adapting to new strategies."

She scribbled another note, then asked, "Do you feel that's something you're applying to other areas of your life?"

He leaned back, contemplating the question. "Yes. Julia and I are working as a team. Even our game nights feel more... purposeful now."

The room was imbued with a sense of calm and clarity, their dialogue building on Ashlee's growing self-awareness.

The therapist's next question was direct yet encouraging. "How do you see your gaming skills helping you resolve real-life challenges?"

Ashlee paused, the answer forming with surprising clarity. "It's like mapping out a level. Breaking down big tasks into smaller, manageable parts."

He recalled the way they'd outlined their schedule at home, how he'd structured his lesson plans at work, even the way he'd approached the gaming session with his friends. Each instance was a testament to his newfound ability to blend digital strategies with real-world needs.

The therapist regarded him with an approving smile. "You're building quite the skill set," she observed. "Do you feel others are noticing?"

Ashlee considered her question, then responded with confidence. "Yes. Julia seems happier. Chen Laoshi even gave me a pat on the shoulder after class."

Her eyes lit up with his quiet triumphs. "How does that recognition impact you?"

"It's validating," Ashlee admitted, a note of surprise in his voice. "It makes me want to keep improving. To keep integrating the things I love with the things that matter."

Their exchange continued with a steady, insightful pace, Ashlee's responses growing more assured as he detailed specific moments of progress.

The session was drawing to a close, but the sense of reflection and growth lingered in the room like the gentle fragrance of tea.

"Any quests you're looking forward to in the coming week?" the therapist asked, a playful tone in her otherwise calm inquiry.

Ashlee chuckled, appreciating her understanding of his world. "Just the usual—conquer home life, keep my students engaged, and try not to get pwned in my next gaming session."

He stood to leave, feeling the support of the session like a soft cloak around him. The therapist watched him go, a satisfied expression on her face.

"See you next time, Ashlee," she called as he reached the door, her voice as warm as the light that filled the inviting space.

He nodded, carrying the positivity of their meeting with him. The challenges ahead seemed less daunting, infused with the skills and strategies he now embraced as strengths.

The serene office closed quietly behind him, but its impact remained, guiding Ashlee with renewed confidence toward a future where his digital past was not just relevant but essential.

XVII

A New Player Enters

Harmony in Dissonance

The living room felt familiar and worn, a space wrapped in cozy comfort. Julia and Ashlee sat close on the sagging sofa, a couple caught between quiet dreams and loud reality. Lamplight pooled softly around them, cradling Julia's warm smile and the earnest, steady gaze she turned on Ashlee. "I'm pregnant," she said, the words landing like a gentle promise. Her hand found Ashlee's arm, a reassuring anchor. His fingers twitched, tiny telltales of an internal conflict. He nodded slowly, eyes flickering between Julia's sure expression and the scattered game manuals on the coffee table. The games were stark reminders of past obsessions, but now, with Julia's announcement, they seemed like remnants of another world. His voice was measured, as though testing unfamiliar terrain. "We've come a long way," he replied.

Julia's grip on Ashlee's arm was light but certain. She squeezed gently, transmitting warmth through the contact. "We have, haven't we?" she agreed, her voice soft and full of knowing. "I wasn't sure when to tell you. But it feels right, doesn't it?" She leaned a little closer, her long, dark hair brushing against Ashlee's shoulder like a comforting shadow.

Ashlee's posture slumped slightly, a physical echo of the thoughts wrestling within. His eyes darted from the couch to the bookshelf, tracing a path over old magazines and novels that Julia had carefully organized but he rarely touched. His world, now suddenly expansive and intimidating, seemed to compress into a single point. "It's—unexpected," he admitted, blinking rapidly. His fingers twitched again, an almost imperceptible movement like a nervous tic. "But... exciting."

Julia smiled at his hesitation, recognizing it as the cautious enthusiasm of a man used to navigating virtual quests, not real-life ones. "We'll navigate this together," she promised, her voice carrying the weight of both assurance and affection. She brushed a stray lock of hair from his forehead, revealing his introspective eyes.

Ashlee felt the sincerity in her words, a balm for his scattered thoughts. He searched her face, looking for doubt, but found none. Instead, he saw hope and determination—qualities he admired but sometimes felt he lacked. "I've been so focused on my little universe," he confessed, his gaze flickering back to the game manuals as though they might disappear any moment. "Maybe too focused."

Julia followed his gaze, understanding his silent admission. "Things change," she said, the hint of a tease in her tone. "Priorities change. But the important things?

They stay the same." Her eyes locked onto his, holding his attention and offering him a lifeline.

Ashlee's brow furrowed slightly as he digested her words. The room felt charged with possibility, each second stretching into a moment of introspection. "Important things like teamwork?" he asked, his tone lighter now, threading through with a nervous humor.

"Exactly," Julia affirmed, her eyes brightening. "I've always admired your strategy skills, you know. But this time, maybe we can write the walkthrough together."

A small smile tugged at Ashlee's lips, tentative but genuine. He felt a warmth rising in his chest, a mix of relief and cautious optimism. The worries that lingered beneath—the fear of new responsibilities, the concern that he might pass on his unique struggles—began to unravel slowly, like a complex puzzle he could solve with patience and support. "I don't want to mess this up," he admitted, his voice tinged with vulnerability.

Julia's expression softened, her gaze never wavering from his. "You won't," she reassured him, speaking with the confidence of someone who had weathered storms and still found the sunshine. "We're in this together, Ashlee. And you're going to be amazing."

The living room seemed to embrace them, its worn edges and cozy clutter forming a backdrop to this new chapter. The moments stretched and twisted, time losing its grip as they lingered in conversation. Ashlee felt his doubts diminish, replaced by a burgeoning sense of purpose. He looked at Julia, the woman who had taken this journey with him and was now offering to forge a new one.

"We've come a long way," he repeated, the words now filled with conviction. Julia's smile mirrored his, wide and sincere, casting the room in a glow that outshone the lamp's soft light.

Together, they leaned back into the cushions, the sofa sagging gently beneath their combined weight. It felt like sinking into something deep and comforting, something safe. Ashlee's hand found Julia's, a small but meaningful gesture that promised so much.

In the quiet that followed, only the soft rustle of paper could be heard as a draft shifted through the game manuals, scattering them further across the coffee table. But neither of them noticed, too engrossed in the world they were beginning to build together. Ashlee's smile lingered, a promise as sure and bright as Julia's announcement had been.

They sat like that for a long time, surrounded by the cozy clutter of their lives, wrapped in the quiet anticipation of what was to come. The responsibilities of parenthood, the thrill of new beginnings, and the comfort of shared dreams filled the room, spilling over the edges like the soft, forgiving light.

Unity of the Dual Self

Later that evening, the kitchen hummed with quiet activity, a place where dreams and practicality shared the same air. Ashlee and Julia moved around the sunlit space, arms filled with baby supplies and planning materials, their enthusiasm almost tangible. The dining table overflowed with notepads, colorful brochures, and a tablet glowing with the latest items on a baby registry. It was organized chaos, the kind that spoke of new beginnings.

Ashlee approached the task like a finely tuned mission, his movements deliberate and precise. "Crib, stroller, car seat," he recited, listing items with the precision of a practiced gamer detailing a strategy. He tapped his pen against the table, marking off a checklist with crisp efficiency. "We're going to need some serious inventory management here."

Julia's gaze swept over the materials, her fingers smoothing creases on a blueprint of the nursery plan. She interjected with practical suggestions, her voice a steady counterpoint to Ashlee's focused rhythm. "And a lifetime supply of diapers," she added, an amused glint in her eyes as she nudged a stack of pamphlets aside to make more room. "We're not speedrunning this, remember?"

The table was a riot of colors and ideas, reflecting their combined excitement and the slightest edge of overwhelm. Notepads filled with Julia's tidy handwriting lay beneath Ashlee's detailed sketches. Brochures advertising the latest baby tech sprawled next to soft, pastel-colored catalogs. The tablet in the center displayed a flickering array of baby registry items, its screen slightly smudged from frequent touches.

Julia glanced at Ashlee, a soft laugh escaping her lips. "Are you planning to unlock achievements with all these supplies?" she teased, arching an eyebrow.

Ashlee grinned, setting his pen down and leaning back to admire their progress. "Maybe," he replied, feigning nonchalance. "I'd say we're close to leveling up."

Before Julia could respond, a friendly nod greeted them from the doorway. Wei Lin entered, placing a small stack of bilingual parenting books next to a set of traditional Chinese baby care guides. "Looks like a boss fight," she observed with gentle humor, taking in the crowded table.

"We're in the early stages," Julia said, flashing a grateful smile at their guest. "Thank you for coming, Wei Lin. And for bringing these." She gestured to the books, her appreciation evident.

Wei Lin settled in smoothly, joining their orbit with an easy familiarity. "Mix what works from the West with what we value here," she suggested, her tone clear and confident. She tapped the cover of a guide, emphasizing her point. "Flexibility is key."

Ashlee nodded, clearly interested in her perspective. He picked up one of the bilingual books, flipping through the pages with curiosity. "I'm guessing we can learn a lot from this approach," he mused, looking at Wei Lin.

She met his gaze with a knowing smile. "I've seen it work," she confirmed. "You know, my own plan was more traditional at first." Her eyes twinkled as she added, "But there's an upgrade path for everything."

Julia laughed, reaching for a notepad to jot down new ideas. "We're learning as we go," she admitted, welcoming the insights. "It's all a bit overwhelming."

Wei Lin's presence added a sense of calm to the room, her advice precise and grounded. "You're doing great already," she encouraged, sorting through the guides she brought. Her fingers moved quickly, picking out one with colorful illustrations. "I recommend this one for your first raid," she joked, the geeky humor not lost on Ashlee.

He smiled, appreciating her understanding. "I've mapped out a preliminary route," he said, gesturing to the various lists and plans on the table. His enthusiasm bubbled just below the surface, infusing his words. "We're going to prioritize essentials and then optimize for comfort."

Julia nodded, picking up where he left off. "And making sure we don't forget the practical stuff," she added, glancing at Ashlee with fond exasperation. "Like laundry detergent."

"Never forget laundry detergent," Wei Lin agreed with mock seriousness, her gentle laughter filling the kitchen. She watched their interaction with a warm smile, clearly enjoying their dynamic.

The three continued their planning, each contributing to the growing complexity and joy of the moment. Hands moved over papers and screens, exchanging ideas and merging suggestions. The kitchen felt alive with energy, a microcosm of shared dreams and anticipated challenges.

"We've got a good raid party going here," Ashlee remarked, feeling the strength of their collaboration. His pen tapped lightly against a page, echoing the lighthearted rhythm of their planning.

Julia's eyes met his, filled with the same sense of adventure that had propelled them this far. "We're ready for anything," she agreed, leaning into Ashlee's shoulder with a contented sigh.

The scene captured their hands moving in concert, laying out the foundations for their future. Wei Lin added the finishing touch, her fingers lingering on a small, cloth-bound journal. "This is for your own notes," she offered, her generosity as understated as always.

Ashlee and Julia exchanged a glance, a shared gratitude evident in their smiles. The kitchen, bright with sun and promise, seemed to embrace them in its warmth, turning their organized chaos into the first step of a beautiful new journey.

XVIII

The Next Level

A Hero's Farewell

Ashlee hunched slightly at the front of his modern classroom, holding a stylus like a saber. Behind him, vivid graphics clashed on the digital whiteboard. "Bam! We got the sword!" he called with glee as the students leaned in, nodding in unison as if part of an elaborate dance move. "How did you do that?" one of them asked, wide-eyed, and Ashlee pushed his glasses up, giving the child an impish look. "What do you think?" he replied, knowing he had them completely hooked. That was when Chen Laoshi appeared in the doorway, arms crossed and smiling like a proud mother hen. "Your innovative approach brings learning to life," she remarked, before glancing at the entranced students. "It appears you've found your audience." Ashlee gave a sheepish grin, the warm afternoon sun wrapping him in a glow.

Ashlee stood there, absorbing the excitement that buzzed through the room like static electricity. The whiteboard continued to light up with colorful explosions as he gestured enthusiastically with his stylus. "This part's a bit tricky," he warned with a grin, as a new puzzle filled the screen. "Who can tell me what happens if we move the red block?" He turned to face the kids, his eyes gleaming with a playful challenge.

The students didn't need to be asked twice. They crowded around the front, some perched on the edges of their seats while others knelt on their chairs. "Move it up!" one shouted, barely able to contain himself. "No, to the side!" another argued, jabbing her finger in the air. "Just try it!" urged a third, his voice squeaking in excitement. Ashlee laughed softly, enjoying the show of enthusiasm.

"Let's see what happens," Ashlee suggested, dragging the block with deliberate slowness across the board. When the puzzle piece locked into place, the screen erupted with fireworks, and the room filled with a chorus of triumphant cheers. "Way to go, team," Ashlee said, his voice warm with pride. He set them up with another challenge, knowing they were now fully immersed in the lesson.

This time, the game presented a more complex task, and Ashlee tapped the stylus rhythmically on the board as he guided the students through it. "Look closely at this part," he told them, zooming in on a tangled mess of colors and shapes. "What do you think our next move should be?"

There was a collective gasp, followed by a storm of ideas and questions. "We have to move the blue block first!" a girl shouted, tugging on her friend's sleeve. "Wait, I see it!" a boy exclaimed, his eyes as big as saucers. Ashlee encouraged them, dropping hints and asking clever questions that let their curiosity take the lead. "Interesting strategy," he said with a teasing smile, "but what happens if we try this?"

He demonstrated a new tactic, and the students huddled closer, whispering and pointing as if watching a magician reveal a secret trick. Then, just as Ashlee paused dramatically, the familiar voice of Chen Laoshi broke through the clamor.

"Ashlee," she said from the doorway, her professional tone softened with admiration, "your innovative approach brings learning to life."

He turned, a look of surprise quickly transforming into a proud grin. "Thank you," he replied, scratching the back of his neck in a shy gesture. Chen Laoshi's compliment felt like a badge of honor, and he wore it with pleasure.

His attention turned back to the lesson, his movements more energetic, fueled by her validation. "Let's tackle this one together," Ashlee encouraged, motioning for them to gather closer. "This puzzle has a twist, but I know we can crack it."

With renewed vigor, Ashlee guided the students through another complex challenge, breaking it down into smaller steps that led to new discoveries. The kids responded eagerly, their hands shooting up and voices overlapping in a friendly competition to solve the next piece. Ashlee let them take turns controlling the action, their confidence building as they connected the game to the learning objectives.

"I get it now!" one exclaimed, his face lighting up with realization. "It's like solving a real mystery!" another chimed in, bouncing in her seat. Ashlee's eyes sparkled as he watched them, enjoying how the room buzzed with the sound of engaged minds at work.

He wrapped up the lesson with a grand finale, leading them through the last challenge with triumphant flair. As the game flashed "Level Complete!" in bold letters, Ashlee and the students shared a moment of celebration, high-fiving and cheering their success.

The warm glow of the afternoon light mingled with the soft luminescence of the screen, casting a cozy spell over the classroom. Ashlee turned, feeling contentment seep into every corner of the room, like sunlight pooling into shadows.

Chen Laoshi lingered, her presence a subtle reminder of Ashlee's unconventional yet effective methods. "You've created quite the buzz here," she observed, nodding approvingly at the still-excited students.

"It's a fun way to learn," Ashlee replied, feeling the truth of it in his bones. He gathered his things as the students slowly began to disperse, talking animatedly about the day's lesson.

Before leaving, Chen Laoshi shared a few more encouraging words. "You have a special talent for this," she said, her voice full of genuine respect.

Ashlee nodded, gratitude in his eyes. "I appreciate that," he told her, feeling a new confidence in his teaching style. The room gradually emptied, the voices fading like an echo, until Ashlee was left alone with his thoughts, savoring the quiet triumph of the day.

Beyond the Screen

That evening, Ashlee perched on a plush rug in the cozy living room, a position familiar to both gamers and Zen monks. Across from him, his daughter sat, clutching her tablet with the solemnity of a quest. The glow from the screen made a halo of her wild hair as she tapped out a rhythm that said she was very close to figuring this out. "Oh!" she exclaimed, the tablet vibrating slightly in her small hands as it acknowledged her victory. Ashlee let out a satisfied sigh, knowing the sound of triumph when he heard it. "Looks like you're on a roll," he said, stretching his legs and enjoying the warmth that wrapped around both their worlds. Julia lounged on the sofa, observing their quiet competition. "She might just be a natural," she remarked, eyes bright with affection. Ashlee met her gaze, sharing a smile filled with wonder at how his old love had passed on to a new generation.

The soft luminescence of the screen reflected off her delicate features, painting her face in shifting shades of blue and green. She remained deeply focused, her big eyes fixed intently on each puzzle as if decoding an ancient mystery. "You've got this," Ashlee whispered encouragingly, leaning in to watch the action unfold.

With each solved puzzle, her contemplative expression burst into bright enthusiasm, accompanied by delighted giggles that filled the room like chimes in the wind. Ashlee returned her joy with a warm smile, his own excitement growing with every victory. He sat back, admiring how naturally she seemed to dive into this new world.

The living room enveloped them in coziness, the soft hum of the game a lullaby of digital chirps. Light from the tablet shimmered in the air, wrapping them in an aura that blurred the lines between the virtual and the real.

Julia watched them from the cushioned sofa, her eyes tender and full of admiration. Her presence added an unspoken warmth to the scene, knitting the family together in this shared moment. She and Ashlee exchanged a knowing look, their thoughts perfectly aligned in amazement at their daughter's intuitive connection to the game.

They both sensed something special, a bridge from past to present forming right before their eyes. Julia's smile deepened, and she pulled a blanket over her legs, content to witness this new chapter unfold.

Ashlee saw a mirror of his own passion in his daughter's intense concentration and boundless curiosity. He thought back to his early days, exploring digital worlds with the same sense of wonder and thrill. Now, watching her navigate these virtual puzzles, he felt a delightful déjà vu.

Her focus remained unwavering as she tapped her way through another challenge, her small hands moving with the dexterity of a seasoned player. "Hmm," she pondered aloud, tilting her head thoughtfully before breaking into another triumphant giggle. The tablet buzzed happily, a faithful companion on her quest.

Ashlee's heart swelled with pride, seeing so much of himself in her determined little figure. The quiet room echoed with the gentle sound of her tapping, punctuated by exclamations of discovery that turned the living room into a theater of new adventures.

Julia finally broke the spell, her voice a gentle tease. "She really is a natural, isn't she?" she said, eyes sparkling as she glanced at Ashlee. He chuckled softly, running a hand through his hair.

"Just like her old man," he replied with a playful grin. "I'd say she's learning pretty quickly."

They continued to watch her, the atmosphere filled with unspoken possibilities. Julia's admiration for Ashlee's nurturing approach was clear in her gaze. She reached for her tea, savoring both the warmth of the cup and the moment.

"Who knows where this might lead?" Julia mused, imagining the paths their daughter could explore. Ashlee nodded, the prospect of future gaming adventures with her igniting a new sense of purpose.

"I think she'll surprise us," he said, eyes soft with love. "This is just the beginning."

Julia's hand found his, a subtle gesture that spoke volumes about their shared dreams. She marveled at how Ashlee's passion had taken root in the next generation, transforming from a solitary pursuit to a cherished family bond.

The conversation flowed easily, as natural as the smiles they exchanged. "Remember when you thought gaming was just a distraction?" Ashlee teased, raising an eyebrow at Julia.

"I still do," she replied with a wink, "but maybe it's a distraction worth having."

Their laughter was soft and full of joy, wrapping around them like the blanket on Julia's lap. They continued to talk about the joy of discovery, the thrill of games, and the wonder of seeing their daughter embrace it all.

The room seemed to glow with a life of its own, each pixel on the tablet a tiny star in the constellation of their family's new adventure. The gentle hum of the game was a comforting presence, a promise of future explorations together.

As their daughter finally settled down, content with her digital victories, Ashlee and Julia watched her with quiet awe. Her eyelids grew heavy, and the tablet slowly slipped from her fingers. Ashlee caught it just in time, smiling at the peaceful sight.

He and Julia shared one last, tender look, knowing that this was only the beginning of many more adventures. The room embraced them in warmth and tranquility, the night unfolding with the soft promise of tomorrow's quests.

Until Next Time